"I don't need a psychological evaluation. I need you."

He was only so much of a saint. In fact, he wasn't a saint at all. "Kendall, you're scared. I understand that. But I'm not the answer."

"I'm not looking for answers." She ran her palms up his back, pressing him closer. "You treat me like a china doll. As if you're afraid of me."

"I'm not—" She did scare the hell out of him. They had nothing in common except Rancho Diablo, which wasn't even his home, or hers.

The problem was how much he wanted her.

"I want you, Sloan."

He didn't reply. In the darkness, Kendall couldn't read his face. He'd tensed up, a hard stone fortress in her arms—but then his lips touched hers, seeking, before turning demanding.

Sparks shattered inside her. She kissed him back, drawing him to her, not about to let him get up on his good-soldier horse and ride away.

Dear Reader,

I love the Callahans, and I'm thrilled you have found a place for them in your hearts, too! The New Year starts off with Sloan's story, as he and his family meet their Callahan cousins at Rancho Diablo. Sloan never dreamed he'd find himself battling to keep the Callahan legacy secure—let alone falling for the beautiful, sexy Kendall Phillips. But the biggest shocker of all for Sloan is discovering how much he loves the idea of being a father, when he never saw himself settling down. How can he resist falling for the woman who makes him realize the last thing he wants is to be a lone wolf?

I hope you enjoy this new chapter in the Callahan saga. This is the first of seven new stories, where the Chacon Callahans are brought into the fold, where love and land intertwine to forge new ties for them all. As we meet these Callahan cousins, it's my fondest wish that you will love, laugh and enjoy their journey home with them.

Best wishes to you all,

Tina

www.tinaleonard.com

www.facebook.com/tinaleonardbooks

A Callahan Outlaw's Twins

TINA LEONARD

HARLEQUIN®

entertain, enrich, inspire™

Recycling programs
for this product may
not exist in your area.

ISBN-13: 978-0-373-75437-3

A CALLAHAN OUTLAW'S TWINS

Copyright © 2013 by Tina Leonard

Printed in U.S.A.

ABOUT THE AUTHOR

Tina Leonard is a *USA TODAY* bestselling and award-winning author of more than fifty projects, including several popular miniseries for Harlequin American Romance. Known for bad-boy heroes and smart, adventurous heroines, her books have made the *USA TODAY*, Waldenbooks, Ingram and Nielsen BookScan bestseller lists. Born on a military base, Tina lived in many states before eventually marrying the boy who did her crayon printing for her in the first grade. You can visit her at www.tinaleonard.com, at www.facebook.com/tinaleonardbooks and www.twitter.com/tina_leonard.

Books by Tina Leonard

HARLEQUIN AMERICAN ROMANCE

Many thanks and much love to the readers who have supported my writing with such devotion and generosity. Your enthusiasm is the reason I write.

Prologue

Chief Running Bear looked out across the canyons as he sat astride a black Diablo mustang. He looked to the east, then the west, and finally northward. A huge plume of dust rose on the horizon, painting the New Mexico sky an ominous gray. The air stirred, unsettled. The chief knew what the signs meant.

What was coming could not be stopped, nor changed. The past was rising to meet them, just as before.

He turned the Diablo mustang south, and they melted into the canyons.

There was no time to waste.

Chapter One

"All I can say is that the Callahans are unafraid to live by their own rules, no matter the consequences. It makes you want to live a little harder yourself. I call it Callahan fire."

—Bode Jenkins, when asked by a reporter
about his neighbors

Sloan Chacon stared at the note tacked to the door of his isolated cabin, an event that had happened three times before in his life. This time it had been placed while he was sleeping. Highly trained and decorated Navy SEALs did not normally find themselves in the presence of someone stealthier than they.

Sloan pulled the note off the rustic wood. It was from Chief Running Bear, the connection to his old life, and his paternal grandfather.

The instructions, as always, were cryptic.

There are many mysteries in a man's life. You are needed now, to protect the family and your heritage. Go to the Callahan ranch in New Mexico. Near the canyons you will find seven large stones,

*one placed for each of you. This ring of stone will
be your home from now on, in your heart.*

He'd known this day was coming, from the day
his parents had left. They'd said "the chief will guide
you"—and they'd disappeared. He and his brothers
and sister had split up, moved in separate directions
when they were old enough. Life in the tribe was over.

He hadn't understood much then. But his parents
had been right: the chief had guided them.

He'd just resented the hell out of it.

JONAS AND SAM CALLAHAN stared across the ranch land
of Rancho Diablo toward the canyons. Jonas lowered
the night-vision binoculars. "I see a circle of seven large
rocks, and a small fire in the center. My guess is it's
the bat signal, with our grandfather starring as Alfred."

"Chief business," Sam said.

Jonas nodded. "The chief's not holding a séance, so
something's up."

Sam took the binoculars. "I knew the peace couldn't
last forever."

Jonas waited for Sam's assessment of the fire and
ring of stone.

"There are eight people. Six dudes, the chief and
what may be a reasonably decent-looking chick with
spiky light hair. Around our age, but hard to tell. They
look fit."

"You mean they look like they're strong enough
to tote diaper bags and baby gear," Jonas said. "I've
bulked up with the nineteen kids on this ranch."

"Exactly. Shall we butt in?"

"I thought you'd never ask."

Sam set the binoculars down. "The chief wouldn't

have let us see him if he didn't want us to know something's going on. That means he expects all of us to show."

"I'm on it," Jonas said, sending a mass text to the brothers.

Cut yourselves loose. Chief situation.

"Here we go," Sam said.

"Ever think what our lives would be like without the chief?" Jonas asked his brother, hearing a rumble of thunder deep in the heart of the canyons that could only be the mystical Diablos running, a portent of things to come.

"Yeah." Sam slid into a leather jacket, stuck a small pistol in the back of his jeans. "Boring as hell."

But boring had been nice for the past year.

SLOAN FOUND THE SPOT easily enough—the small fire was an excellent marker. He put his pack down and eyed the dark landscape around him, checking for danger. His heart beat hard, adrenaline kicking in. "You can come out. Let's get this party started."

His five brothers slowly materialized from the shadows. Sloan waited. A few seconds passed, then his slightly built sister stepped close to the fire.

"I'm here. *Now* the party can get rocking," Ashlyn said.

They embraced each other. Cold night air blew down his jacket collar, but Sloan didn't care. It felt too good to be with his family again. They'd waited a long time for this moment.

He wished they could stay together forever.

But they weren't alone. Sloan stood still as six tall

men appeared out of the darkness like night specters. The two groups stared across the fire, sizing each other up.

Sloan had no idea how long the chief had been standing next to him. His grandfather's face gave away nothing, and Sloan wondered why they'd all been called to this remote location.

"This is Callahan land," the chief said. "You are all Callahans."

Sloan looked at the impassive faces gathered around the fire. If this was family, it felt very strange to learn about it now. "We are Chacon."

"Chacon Callahan. You are related by blood. Your fathers are brothers." The chief met the gaze of each of them in turn. "One of you is the hunted one."

Sloan stared at the chief. "What does that mean, hunted?"

"It means one may die if the thirteen do not work together. No matter what, nothing can separate you from your purpose."

"Which is what?" Sloan demanded.

"Protecting the family." The chief looked at Jonas.

"Is there another mercenary coming?" Jonas asked.

"There was never only one," the chief said. "You knew they would send more. They are nearing Rancho Diablo even as we speak."

"If these guys have a problem, what does that have to do with us?" Sloan asked.

"Callahan is Callahan. The fight is the same." The chief gestured one last time at the clan gathered in a circle. "Get to know each other well. A single stick can be broken, but a bundle not so easily."

"I've heard that before," Sloan said. "Any further intel would be appreciated."

"Your home is here," the chief said. "Keep the ring of stone and fire in your hearts. Across the canyons, a few miles as the eagles flies, lies danger."

"If we're supposed to be a bundle," Jonas said, "I assume they're staying with us at Rancho Diablo? They're welcome to, of course, though we can take care of ourselves."

"For now they stay here." The chief squatted next to the fire, waved a hand over it. "You have nineteen children, six wives and two elderly people on the ranch, Jonas. It is best to have your cousins remain in this place so they can keep a lookout."

"I'd watch calling Aunt Fiona and Uncle Burke elderly," Jonas replied. "Chief, we can establish our own lookouts." He glanced across the fire at his new kin.

Sloan knew exactly how Jonas felt. "Why again is this our problem?"

"Brother takes care of brother." The chief let that sink in for a moment. "Remember that only blood matters. Stay together and yet separate. There is strength in all of you, but even a chain can be broken if the weakest link is not reinforced," the chief said, rising. "Here the past and the future become one. What comes now will change you all."

He disappeared, and the fire dimmed. Hoofbeats echoed eerily in the darkness.

Sloan had little patience for open-ended missions with little purpose, and slackers who couldn't take care of themselves. He appointed himself troubleshooter, deciding to go ahead and shoot this trouble in the head before it took over their lives. "I take it you're in some kind of jam, cousins," he said. "Not really sure we can help you."

"I'm Jonas Callahan. And as far as I knew when I

woke up this morning, the only jam in my world was on my toast. We thought we were doing just fine until you showed up."

Sloan took the hand stretched out to him, giving it a brief shake. "Sloan. These are my brothers and sister. Falcon, Galen, Jace, Dante, Tighe and Ashlyn."

Ashlyn's diminutive size caught Jonas's attention. He glanced at Sloan.

"She's not the weak link," Sloan said drily. "Trust me on that. Five feet two of meanness if you cross her."

"Good," Jonas said. "No offense, Ashlyn."

"Not a problem," she said.

Jonas looked at Sloan. "These are my brothers. Creed, Pete, Sam, Rafe and Judah."

"Seven of us, six of you?" Sloan asked.

"Guess your father was more prolific," Jonas said.

"Or he was determined to have a girl," Ashlyn said, her tone sweet.

Jonas eyed Sloan. "We'll head on now."

He nodded. Sloan glanced around at the rest of the Callahans on the opposite side of the fire. There was definitely a strong resemblance, but they didn't feel like family.

Yet they were supposed to fight for a common cause, against something dangerous that affected all of them.

Sloan didn't get it. Frankly, if the seven of them had been brought in to help these six, he wasn't all that interested.

His family could stand on their own.

Too bad if theirs couldn't.

Chapter Two

Kendall Phillips looked down at the sleeping man, unsure how to wake him. He slept like he was dead, which he probably should be, considering he'd spent the night on the ground at Rancho Diablo. In the not-quite-dawn light, she saw that the fire had gone out, perhaps hours ago.

The next thing Kendall knew, she was flat on her backside in the dust. "Ow!" Her fanny smarted—and now this guest of Jonas's was on her *very bad* side. "Let go of me, you gorilla!"

"Who are you? What are you doing here?" he demanded.

She noted he didn't release her, and she squelched the great desire to pull off one of her high-heeled Manolo Blahniks and pierce him with it. "I'm Kendall Phillips. I was sent with coffee and to bring you in to meet the family while it's still dark. Let go of my ankle!"

She slapped his hand, but he didn't seem to mind. He slowly released her, his fingers lingering against her skin—as if he wasn't used to feeling anything soft.

Chills ran up her legs.

"Sorry," he said. "Not used to a chuck wagon showing up to greet me, nor a female."

Kendall stood, turning to look at her white Chanel skirt, which now bore a target-size dirt mark on it, very visible despite the dimness still covering the ranch. "Apology not accepted. I was trying to wake you gently, you..." She sized the man up as he stood. "You do look like a Callahan."

"That's because I am." He glanced around. "Do me a favor. Don't tell my brothers and sister you made it to the fire without me taking you out."

"I beg your pardon," Kendall said, "but I can assure you that you and I will never be going out."

"It's okay. We had a bead on her all along," a female voice said. Five large men and one much smaller woman appeared out of the darkness. Kendall thought it was amazing how silently they could move.

"You sleep like a bear in winter," the petite blonde said to her brother, who looked embarrassed at her comment. "If she can sneak up on us in those shoes, you're going to stink as a lookout. That's got to change."

"This is all very nice, but not my issue," Kendall said. "Do you want coffee or not?" She put full-force attitude into her voice, letting these people know that she might have gotten dumped on her butt, but it wouldn't happen again.

"Sure," the blonde said. "You're kind of fancy for a rancher, aren't you?"

Kendall was about to let her have it—she hadn't driven a military jeep out to the corner of nowhere to put up with this—but just then her twin brother, Xav, rode up on his big stallion, and the little blonde's eyes went huge in her face.

"Everything all right, Kendall?" Xav asked.

She nodded. "We're getting to know each other, all of us," she said, her gaze on the man who'd spilled her on the ground. "It may take a while. We have different methods of saying hello."

Sloan shrugged. "Where's the coffee, Barbie?"

Kendall sucked in a breath. "Did you just call me *Barbie?*"

The big man looked at her curiously. "Is that a problem?"

His brothers shifted, and as slight streaks of dawn began slowly lighting the sky, she realized that all these people looked *very* Callahan—and a little dangerous.

Darn Jonas for saddling me with this mission.

"My name is Kendall Phillips," she said. "This is my twin, Xavier. We help out at the Callahan ranches."

"Not dressed like that, you don't," Sloan said. "Unless you're the party planner."

"That's right," Kendall said. "That's what I am, the party planner." She glared at him, not caring that he was disgustingly handsome even after sleeping on the ground all night. "You're going to miss the party if you don't all introduce yourselves, because I'm going to drive off in the only mode of vehicular transportation that can make it out here, with your stupid pot of coffee. And you won't eat the hot bacon and eggs Fiona Callahan has waiting on the stove. You don't really know what you'll be missing," she added. "I've done my job. The *party planner's* jeep leaves in five seconds."

"Sloan, Tighe, Dante, Falcon, Galen, Jace and Ashlyn," Sloan said. "Since we need cover of darkness, we'd better get a move on."

He had a nice voice. A little rough and gravelly, maybe, but she thought he'd be appealing if he relaxed.

He didn't look as if he relaxed much. "Can't they speak for themselves?" Kendall demanded.

"Kendall," Xav said, laughing, still astride his horse, "cut them a break. They're not aware of the game rules."

"Yes, we are," Ashlyn said to Xav. "We make the rules."

"Great," Kendall said. "Nothing but fun times ahead, I can tell."

Sloan looked at her. "We appreciate you coming out here. We just weren't expecting company."

She nodded, backing off just a bit. "Let's get you that coffee."

He smiled, and the effect was devastatingly, hauntingly beautiful. As if he didn't smile often, so when he did, the smile came from deep in his soul. Kendall caught her breath—and then remembered that when he'd held her ankle in his strong hand, capturing her, she was pretty certain his fingers had stroked her skin as he'd finally released her.

It had felt nice.

"Sorry about your skirt," he told her. "I'd brush it off, but I think the dirt—"

"Don't you *dare,*" Kendall said. The thought of him brushing her fanny with his big, rough hand alarmed her. It didn't ring a long-forgotten bell of sexual desire at all. "I mean, thank you, it will be fine. Nothing the dry cleaners can't handle."

His dark eyes squinted at the corners, as if he might be trying to smile again but the action was just too rusty for the muscles to obey. He ran a hand through his messy dark hair, waiting for her to lead the way.

Kendall marched the procession to the jeep and the coffee, more than ready to hand the big man and his rowdy band off to Jonas.

Party planner, my foot. Barbie?
What an arrogant devil. Cute, though, I suppose.
If one likes their men rough and tough—and I don't.

THEY FILED SILENTLY into their cousin's house, some-what awed by their surroundings. Their grandfather had said Rancho Diablo was five thousand acres, but it felt bigger. A couple of small oil derricks worked in the distance. The house was Tudor, almost British in style, supposedly Jeremiah Callahan's dream house. Sloan couldn't think of his family as having anything in common with these Callahans. He was pretty certain none of his family had ever been in anything like this joint. There were seven chimneys, for Pete's sake. It was like a ghostly castle rising up off the New Mexico landscape, banked by dark spools of canyons.

A small, gray-haired woman stood at the door to greet them. She wore green rubber boots appropriate for walking in mud or to the barns and a pink apron with red hearts fashioned into the fabric. The apron looked as if it might have been made by small hands in a school project. Sloan thought it had probably been made by one of the many children he'd been warned were here, a veritable army all their own.

But on this cold early morning the ranch was silent except for workers he could see in the distance.

"Come in," the woman said. "I'm your aunt Fiona. Welcome to Rancho Diablo."

Sloan and his siblings went into a grand foyer in which a massive iron chandelier hung overhead. He glanced at the others, who shrugged at him.

"It's not home," Ashlyn said, "but it's not bad, either."

"Follow me," Fiona said cheerfully. "I'm sure you're

cold and hungry. The chief says I can only keep you here an hour before you must depart." They trailed after her into a large kitchen where the fragrance of eggs and coffee and toast permeated the room. Sloan's stomach rumbled to get at the food.

He glanced at Kendall. Now that they were in a well-lit room, he realized the dirt mark on her skirt was huge. That spot was never coming out without professional assistance. Of course, the spot only made him realize what a really nice fanny she was packing.

"I have to admit that the chief pulled a shocker on me. Still, we're always delighted to have family about. Rancho Diablo is a family place." Fiona looked around the room with a smile. "In the future, Kendall will be your liaison. Anything you need, you let her know. Grab a plate and tell me your name as you fill up," the older woman said. "This is dine and dash, I'm afraid. We're just lucky it's the darkest part of the year. It gives you a little more time."

Sloan's gaze went to Kendall's. She raised a shoulder as if to say, "You blew your shot with me, dude. Don't look my way."

His brothers and sister wasted no time taking their plates and introducing themselves to Fiona and her husband, Burke, as they went by in the line. Sloan went over to talk to Kendall, hoping to make amends.

"Let me pay for cleaning the skirt."

She wrinkled her nose. "Don't worry about it."

"Stubborn."

"You should talk." She gestured toward the food. "One thing you'll learn about being around this branch of the Callahan family tree—if you're hungry, you'd best get to the front of the line. The men in this group eat. Last one in line gets a short stack."

He grinned. "I'm not used to eating a lot."

Her gaze floated down his body. "You're thin," she agreed. "All the same, this is the only food you'll get for a while."

"It's fine. There's always something to eat."

"Not unless you like snake." She grabbed a plate, handing it to him. "I don't eat snake, so I'm going to eat your share if you don't get a move on."

He didn't have to be told twice. He let Fiona fill his plate, murmured his thanks and seated himself at the long table with everyone else.

"This is very nice of you," Ashlyn said. "Thank you, Fiona."

"I don't understand," she replied, "why you can't just stay on this ranch." She studied the group. "Jonas! Why can't they stay here? Why is the chief complicating things? If we need protection, shouldn't they be here? We certainly have the room," Fiona muttered. "It's twenty-nine degrees outside, for heaven's sake, well below freezing."

Jonas pulled up a chair near his aunt, shrugged at his cousins. "If I had a dime for every time someone tried to figure out the chief, I'd be a wealthy man."

Fiona sniffed. "You are a wealthy man, don't be an ass. Now," she said, staring straight at Sloan, "wouldn't you rather stay here than out in the cold?"

He gulped his coffee. "Ma'am, I'm just following orders."

Fiona frowned. "Good soldier."

Kendall met his gaze, blinking. A good soldier probably wouldn't keep staring at the pretty ranch employee.

"It's okay," Ashlyn said hurriedly. "We're used to surviving in remote locations. We wouldn't feel right staying here. It's not our assignment."

"Assignment!" Fiona glanced around the table. "You're family! Burke's never going to rest knowing you're all out there sleeping on the hard ground. He's going to think he needs to join you."

With an under-her-breath murmur, Fiona cracked more eggs into a bowl. Sloan tried not to shovel food into his mouth. He was hungrier than he wanted to let on, and this was the best food he'd had in a long time.

Kendall brought a basket of muffins to the table, sliding in next to him.

"Chocolate chip or blueberry? Fresh-baked, so take your pick. Then pass the basket."

He did exactly as she told him, although with Kendall sitting next to him, his attention was on her instead of the muffins.

Okay, so she was hot. He'd seen hot before. The worst thing he could do was mess up a mission by thinking the woman next to him was hotter than the muffin he'd just deposited on his plate. He passed the basket, gulped some orange juice. "Thanks."

"Don't thank me, thank Fiona. She was suffering last night, worrying about your family out there in the cold." Kendall didn't look at him. "We baked muffins this morning to take her mind off things. It was the only way I could calm her down. Anyway, we had no idea you were coming here until the chief showed up, so please feel free to share any details you'd like to."

Fiona stopped stirring to listen. Jonas glanced over with curiosity. Sam, Rafe, Creed, Pete and Judah had draped themselves over different spots in the kitchen, surreptitiously eyeing their new cousins. Sloan felt the men looking at them, trying not to stare, but the tension was thick as canyon dust.

"Sure," Ashlyn said. "I'm the youngest. I'd like to

say it was hard being the youngest, and the only girl in a family of men, but I'm harder on them than they are on me." She smiled. "I'll do the other introductions, because my big brothers are modest and you won't get much out of them."

Polite laughter from the other Callahans met his sister's words. Sloan was just glad for the chance to eat, if Ashlyn was going to do the chatting. Kendall picked at a biscuit and sipped some water, and Sloan thought she seemed anxious about something. Then again, maybe she was one of those women who didn't eat much and ran on nervous energy. He gazed at her, trying to define her aura. She glanced at him, and he realized she'd thought he was staring at her. Which he was, but not because he was attracted to her or anything. Definitely not.

Although she was quite beautiful, in a polished, cosmopolitan sort of way. Silver water to his family's rough stone darkness.

"That's Galen over there," Ashlyn said. "He's the oldest, thirty-five. He's a hard-ass and a daredevil at times, but he's a great guy to have at your back."

"Easy, sis," Galen said. "They don't want a bio on us."

"It's not name, rank and serial number," Ashlyn retorted. "This is long-lost family."

Silence met Ashlyn's comment. Sloan cleared his throat.

"Jonas is eldest at Rancho Diablo," Kendall said. "He's my direct boss, and something of a nerd. He has a darling wife named Sabrina, whom he worked very hard to win."

Sloan examined the eldest Callahan, a little surprised when Jonas laughed easily at Kendall's words. The tension in the room evaporated just a bit.

"I don't know if I've won Sabrina yet," Jonas said, "but I'm trying."

Sloan thought that was an amazing sentiment. He hadn't had a serious relationship in so many years that he felt a little pang at the difference in their circumstances. What must it be like to live in this mansion, on this enormous ranch, with a wife and kids you adored?

"Falcon's thirty-three," Ashlyn continued. The brother in question inclined his head to Kendall, then looked around at his new cousins. "Falcon's a bit wacky. He's smart as hell. Can wear you out with minutia. Loves puzzles. Will go off for days when he's thinking about something." She grinned at him. "Isn't that right, Falcon?"

Falcon grunted at his sister, who was delighted with her teasing. Sloan squirmed a bit, knowing he was up next on the roll call. No one could ever be certain what Ashlyn was going to say.

"Sloan's my hero," Ashlyn told Kendall. "He's third in the family tree, thirty-one years of loner tough guy. Can go for months without talking, can't you, Sloan?" she asked, winking at him.

"Not months," Sloan said.

"Okay, he'll allot himself a word a day." Ashlyn shot him a gleeful look. "He's picked up a few decorations, is a really good shot with just about any gun on the planet—"

"That's enough," Sloan said. "They don't want to hear everything about me."

Beside him, he could feel Kendall's eyes on him. "I don't know," she said. "It can't hurt to know more about the family I'm in charge of. Every detail helps."

He looked at her. "In charge of?"

Kendall nodded. "Jonas has assigned me to seeing to your family's comfort. 'Liaison' really means 'take care of.'"

"Here's the thing," Sloan said, addressing his remarks to Jonas, but looking at Kendall, since he just couldn't seem to help himself. "We don't need anyone assigned to us for our comfort. No offense, Kendall."

"None taken," Kendall said. "I'm just following orders."

He recognized his own words coming back to him. "We can survive no matter the terrain, and you wouldn't see us for six months."

"That's kind of creepy, though a great talent," Kendall said. "Jonas, this is your call."

Sloan wasn't certain how he felt about the tiny doll calling him creepy. He glanced around at his brothers and sister, puzzled.

"It is creepy," Falcon said. "I mean, when you think about it, on the surface."

Ashlyn laughed. "Actually, it's not creepy to Sloan. He likes roughing it. When we were kids—"

Sloan put down his napkin and pushed back his chair. "Fiona, thank you kindly for breakfast. It was delicious."

His brothers nodded in agreement.

"Jonas, can I talk to you? Privately?" Sloan asked.

"Sure," Jonas said.

Kendall watched the two big men go off together. "Well," she said, "Mr. Stoic certainly wants to talk now."

Ashlyn craned her head to stare after Sloan, who'd cornered Jonas in the den. "He's going to be hard to drag in from the cold. Me, I'm never going to pass up delicious food."

Fiona smiled at her. "I'll put some meat on your bones."

Kendall laughed at Ashlyn's perplexed expression. "Fiona wants to put meat on everyone's bones."

"Okay," Ashlyn said. "If you think you can, I won't say no."

"I won't, either." One of the Callahans who hadn't gotten an introduction yet reached across the table to shake Kendall's hand. "I'm Jace. Sorry about my brother's rudeness. He's pretty much the lone wolf in the family."

Kendall sneaked a peek into the den at the lone wolf. As wolves went, Sloan wasn't all that feral. In fact, he was darn handsome, even better than she'd originally realized, now that she could see him in good light. "Hi, Jace. It's nice to meet you."

"Jace is our earth soul," Ashlyn said. "He's about to hit the big three-o, so he spends a fair amount of time with the ladies."

"Ash," Jace said, "it's all friendly. Although, if you have a sister, Kendall…"

Everyone laughed at Jace's obvious hint to Kendall. She felt herself blush a bit.

"No sister. Sorry. It's just me and three brothers. You'll meet them soon enough."

"Your twin, Xavier, came out to our campsite with you this morning," Ashlyn said.

Kendall nodded. "And then there's Gage and Shaman. They're around here somewhere, probably out feeding the horses at this hour."

"Don't mind Sloan." Another Callahan reached over to offer his hand. "He's a little harder to get to know than the rest of us. I'm Tighe, by the way, and Dante here is my twin."

Hot as the dickens, both of them. Kendall shook their hands, ignoring the words about not minding Sloan. Why should she? She didn't know any of them. Getting bent out of shape about Sloan's obvious prickliness would be unprofessional.

"Wild at heart," Ashlyn said, pointing her fork at Tighe, "will never settle down. A shame, because he'd make a great husband for some lucky woman, and that's not just a sister's pride talking."

Kendall smiled at Tighe. "Be warned that men seem to drop like flies around here, if you're really determined to hang on to your bachelor status. Fiona has a major matchmaking streak going."

Tighe went a little pale. "I'll keep that in mind."

"And Dante," Ashlyn said, "let's just say that he's the head of mischief in our family. Great to have at your side in a fight, but isn't above letting you sweat it out, either. And if you don't like snakes or other creepy-crawlies, don't tell him. He'll put them in your bed just to give you a little fright."

Kendall leveled round eyes on Dante. "Remember I hold the key to the breakfasts, Dante."

He laughed. "You're safe."

Sloan slid back into the seat next to her.

"Get it all worked out?" Kendall asked.

He looked at her. "Jonas has pointed out a few things I was overlooking."

Kendall smiled. "So you're stuck with me."

His lips twisted. "It appears that way."

"I won't wear any more white skirts around you." Kendall sipped her coffee, her expression innocent.

"You'll stay in good enough condition as long as you don't sneak up on me," Sloan said.

"I'll wear a bell around my neck," Kendall said, and Ashlyn said, "That won't be necessary. Now that you've caught Sloan napping, you'll never get within a hundred feet of him again without him knowing."

Annoyance crossed Sloan's face. "I wasn't expecting a woman to sneak into camp."

His brothers stared at him. Sloan looked a bit edgy. Kendall went back to picking at her food, not certain why Sloan didn't seem to like her. But he didn't, that was clear as day. Jonas glanced her way, shrugging.

There was nothing that could be done about it. They were all going to have to get along, one big happy family, until whatever reason these new Callahans had been sent here no longer existed.

"It's so nice to meet all of you," Kendall said politely. "Welcome to Rancho Diablo." She went to help Fiona clean the kitchen. This was just a job, and if she was a pain in Sloan's hiney for some reason, then the feeling was certainly mutual.

Chapter Three

Two days later, Kendall stood at the far end of Rancho Diablo, snapping photos of the location where Jonas wanted his new bunkhouse. It was to be a big one, with almost twenty rooms. Two stories high. It would be built well away from the main house, to give everyone a bit more space. With five thousand acres, Jonas had the land to spread out, but this project was big, even by Callahan standards. It was almost an apartment complex, and Kendall looked forward to helping decorate the abode.

Gazing to the west, she noticed something strange—seven stones placed in a circle near the same location where the bunkhouse was planned. She checked her notes again, making certain she had the correct aerial photographs and surveyor's map, before realizing that this was exactly where Sloan had been sleeping. The large gray-white rocks were about fifty yards away.

A shadow crossed her, briefly blocking the sun on the already cold November day. A tingle touched her skin. She put the camera back up to her face to snap another photo, feeling suddenly nervous about being this far from the main house. She knew the Callahan cousins might be around here somewhere. Still, something made her feel…uncomfortable.

She heard a noise that sounded much like a rock dropping behind her. But the area where she stood was dotted with little more than the odd cactus. Possibly a bird had landed and then flown away.

No. The shadow had been too large to be a cloud or even a bird. Goose pimples rose on her arms, and she began to walk quickly toward the jeep. Something jumped out of nowhere, ramming the jeep as she got in. It slashed at her calf and Kendall shrieked, tossing her camera into the passenger seat and jamming her keys into the ignition. Gunning the engine, she shot away from the stone ring, spraying sand and dirt in her retreat, her only thought to get back to the ranch.

"Whoa!" Sloan shouted. She'd nearly run him over as he was leaving the main house. Kendall jammed the jeep into Park and jumped out into his arms.

"Uh, Barbie," Sloan said. "To what do I owe the pleasure?"

Kendall shivered, laying her head against his chest for just a second as she caught her breath. "I don't know."

"Good," Sloan said. He rubbed her back. "Nice to know you're not just trying to run me down."

She pulled away, his joke fortifying her. "If you ever call me Barbie again, I will stab you with the nearest sharp object. And you won't like it."

"I know." He laughed, setting her away from him. "I've got to go, beautiful. Are you going to be all right?"

She took a deep breath. "I'm fine."

"You don't look like you're fine." He gazed at her closely. "What the hell happened?"

"There was something there." Kendall tried to remember, forcing herself to think beyond her panic. "I don't know. There was a shadow, and then...something attacked the jeep." She glanced down at her leg.

Sloan knelt to look at her calf, squinting as he ran a gentle hand along her bare skin. "Let's get you inside where I can see it better."

Kendall's teeth began a nervous staccato chatter. "You're not supposed to be here in daylight. You'd better go."

"We're not bats," he said wryly. "Besides, apparently Fiona worked her magic on the chief. We're staying in the bunkhouse now."

"Here?" Kendall blinked. "You're not going to be the secret Callahans anymore?"

He nodded. "Come on. More walking, less chat. I'll explain everything when we get inside."

"You're bossy." She followed until he scooped her into his arms, which she started to protest, until she realized she was shaking and had lost a shoe. "I'm not helpless."

"I know. Humor me."

He was just like Jonas. "I don't understand. What could Fiona possibly have said that changed things with Running Bear?" Kendall tried not to focus on how strong Sloan was, and the fact that she could feel impressive muscles in the arms wrapped tightly around her.

"Let's worry about your leg." He took her inside the house, and she didn't complain anymore, feeling a bit woozy.

"What happened?" Fiona asked, coming over with Jonas to look at her leg.

"I don't know exactly." Kendall leaned in to see what everyone was staring at as Sloan laid her carefully on the sofa. He tried to lean her back against the pillows and she waved him away. "Oh, my. That is not pretty."

"What got you?" Sloan asked, peering closely at her skin.

She wasn't sure she liked being the object of so much of his attention. "I'm not sure. It happened so fast."

Sloan looked up at Jonas. "Can you call my brother Galen? We might as well let the doctor take a look at this." He smiled. "He's actually a pretty good medicine man."

There was a good deal of blood running down her leg. Kendall glanced at Fiona. "May I borrow a towel, please? I don't want to bleed on the sofa."

"You poor thing!" Fiona exclaimed, running to fetch one as Jonas went to yell for Galen.

"Jonas is a doctor. He can figure out if anything is wrong." Kendall looked closely at her leg, and felt a little faint seeing her own blood. There was so much. She'd thought perhaps it was a scratch, but now realized the tear was long and angry.

"Jonas is a cardiac guy," Sloan said. "Galen is an internist. And a spirit healer, by the way."

Kendall sniffed. "There is nothing wrong with my spirit. Just my pride. I must have scraped myself when I jumped in the jeep."

Jonas came back with Galen, and Fiona handed him a thick fluffy towel and some antiseptic. Galen smiled reassuringly at Kendall before bending to examine her leg.

"Sloan," Galen said, peering at the wound.

Sloan looked at Kendall, who frowned back at him with some suspicion. "I don't think so," he said to Galen.

Galen looked at Kendall's leg again. "Do it."

Sloan squatted, placed his palms on either side of the wound.

"What's he doing?" Kendall demanded, glancing at Jonas, who shrugged.

"Energy transfer," Galen said helpfully, as if she'd know what that meant. "A little touch therapy in this case. It won't take long."

She wasn't sure she liked having Sloan's slightly rough palms on her calf and knee. His big hands surrounded the injury without touching it. Closing his eyes, he took a deep breath.

"It's really not that big a deal," Kendall said. "A bandage ought to do the trick. Maybe a little iodine or something." She looked at Fiona helplessly, suddenly afraid. For whatever reason, the two brothers acted as if her injury was so serious. "Could have been a wolf, I guess," she said slowly, knowing very well that something huge had hit the jeep. Something that had meant to harm her.

A little of the shock began to wear off as Sloan cupped her ankle, sliding his hands back up her calf, his eyes still closed. "Whatever it was, it was big, though I'm not trying to exaggerate." Sloan's palms warmed her, and she could have sworn she felt pulses of electricity emitting from him into her skin. Even deeper, into her muscles.

His eyes opened, and she found herself gazing into them. "What is it?" she asked.

"Not a thing," Sloan said. "Everything is fine. A little rest will make you feel a lot better. *Rest.* You will wake up soon, and all will be well." He slowly moved his hand in a circular motion in front of her face, and that was the last thing Kendall remembered.

"I KNOW IT'S A HUMAN attack, but what else can you discern?" Galen asked as Sloan carefully eased Kendall's head back onto a pillow so she could sleep comfortably. He estimated that between the shock and the blood loss, the hypnosis might keep her out for an hour—hopefully long enough to get her to the hospital.

"This is a knife injury." Sloan pointed to specific areas of Kendall's leg. "As Galen said, this wasn't done by an animal or even by Kendall scraping herself on something on the jeep. You can sense the dark power radiating here and here," he said, pointing for Jonas's and Fiona's benefit. "My guess is that they were planning to take her hostage."

It bothered him to say that. Kendall was a free spirit. And delicate. Maybe too delicate to survive on this ranch now.

"How can you tell all that just from looking at her leg?" Jonas demanded.

Sloan shrugged. "It's in between what she said and what she didn't say happened. What she remembers and what her subconscious recalls. Put your hands here," he told Jonas, "and you can feel more. Notice the smooth cut in the skin, which indicates a sharp edge of some kind. Very likely a knife. But here, where her skin is torn, you'll note a slashing and tearing effect. Jagged. As you probably know, that has the markings of a military weapon. Something a commando might carry."

Jonas looked at him. "And the rest of the oogie-boogie?"

Sloan smiled. "Close your eyes. See what you see."

Though he appeared doubtful, Jonas placed his hands where Sloan had, and closed his eyes.

He opened them after a moment, shaking his head.

"I don't see anything. I feel warmth in her skin, like infection might be threatening."

Sloan nodded. "That, too. You'll need to ascertain when she had her last tetanus shot. Galen can handle the stitch-up and bandaging."

He stood, not wanting any part of stitching up Kendall. A woman like her who wore figure-hugging suits and sky-high, parrot-colored heels probably wouldn't be pleased with the cosmetic results, though Galen was very good with a needle.

Galen wrapped Kendall's leg efficiently. "I don't want to do it," he said. "She's not going to thank whoever does the surgery."

Sloan nodded. "Wise decision." He looked at Jonas. "You should take her to your local hospital, but be prepared to answer questions, based on the severity of the injury."

Jonas nodded. "I can take her."

"Oh, my," Fiona said. "I don't think anyone knew that the danger was this close. Poor Kendall!"

Sloan looked at the sleeping woman and her now-bandaged leg. Blood would soak through fast enough. Kendall would likely be annoyed when she awakened; it didn't take someone skilled in touch therapy to sense the general impatience and suffer-no-fools sentiment in her personality. And she was brave as hell for going through what had happened without panicking.

"I'll come with you," Sloan told his cousin. "Just in case."

"Just in case what?" Jonas said. "This is Kendall. She's gentle as a summer day."

Sloan smiled. "You want to be the only one around when she wakes up at a hospital with stitches in her pretty leg?"

Jonas looked a bit unhappy. "I guess not."

"Neither would I." Sloan picked Kendall up gently, placing her against his chest and carrying her outside. He settled her carefully in the seat of the sedan Jonas had brought around. They got in and shut the doors.

"So you're really riding along to make sure nothing else happens to her," Jonas said. "You're certain of your kidnapping theory, aren't you?"

He was surprised his cousin had picked up more than he said. "I think she's an easy target."

"You don't know Kendall very well."

This was true. "Her size, her general innocence, lends your employee a vulnerable air."

Jonas sped onto the main road. "She's not very vulnerable."

But she wasn't prepared for whatever was determined to get to the Callahans, either. "She's vulnerable," Sloan said, "and she's not as sweet as you're painting her. I didn't see you raising your hand to stitch her up."

Jonas smiled. "True."

"So don't try to sell me on your employee," Sloan said, "because I'm not buying."

"Just checking," Jonas said.

Sloan was glad to see that they were soon pulling into a community hospital parking lot. "I'll stay outside."

Jonas got out, indicating he needed a wheelchair and assistance from the emergency staff. "You sure?"

"Yeah." Sloan looked at Kendall as she was gently placed into the wheelchair. "Good luck."

Jonas grimaced and went off. Sloan glanced around the hospital grounds, looking for shadows. He figured one would be there somewhere. Whoever attacked Kendall knew they'd gotten in a good hit; they'd be expecting her to show up at the E.R. It was another reason he hadn't pressed Galen to do the stitch-up. Sloan wanted to get a look at whoever was planted at the ranch, before they realized the Diablo Callahans had reinforcements. He hoped to get the jump on them.

He pulled his hat down low and tugged his bandanna up a little more around his neck, and waited.

Chapter Four

Kendall woke up, not happy with Callahans in general, whether Rancho Diablo Callahans or the Callahan cousins. Jonas and Sloan were both on her bad list. "Ouch."

"Only nine stitches," Jonas told her.

"Nine?" She lifted her knee to peer at her calf. "Guess I'm lucky." Fear seeped back into her as she remembered the rush of something dark and sinister coming at her…

"You're lucky." Jonas sat next to her on the hospital gurney. "No more hanging out alone for you."

"What do you mean?" Kendall was outraged. "You sound like Sloan. Where is he?" She glanced around. "I have something to discuss with him. Specifically, that hypnotism thing he pulled on me. Like I'm a baby that needs a nap to calm down."

Jonas grinned. "He's in the parking lot."

"Doing what?" She glared at Jonas.

"Waiting on you. Let's go." He helped Kendall off the gurney and walked her slowly outside.

Sloan was near the E.R. doors, just as Jonas had said. He looked as if he was on security detail, alert, watchful and dangerous—and Kendall realized Sloan was looking for something. Someone.

"You don't think it was an accident, do you?" She got in the car, and Sloan slid in next to her.

"No. How's the leg?"

It hurt. "Never mind. I'll live." She moved to get a bit more comfortable on the seat, and Sloan pulled her leg across his lap.

"Keep it up to help the swelling," Sloan said.

She wanted to argue, but it did feel better to have her leg elevated. His fingers on her ankle, keeping her leg steady, were warm and comforting. Kendall sighed as a wave of tiredness swept over her. "Look, Callahan, you and I are going to have words in the very near future."

He smiled, and she closed her eyes. He didn't seem as worried as he should be about her temper. It was a strange thing. She was in charge of a global company that made and shipped large construction equipment. Her phone rang constantly with business deals. But Sloan seemed to think she was a helpless woman.

I've got a lot to discuss with that handsome rebel. Male chauvinists are not an attractive species.

But right now, he seemed pretty nice. His hand felt good on her ankle, and she knew she should chew his butt, but for some reason, her leg seemed to hurt less now that he was touching her.

I'll seriously bawl him out tomorrow.

Jonas, too.

THE MEETING THAT NIGHT was held in the immense and beautiful upstairs library at Rancho Diablo, apparently a Callahan tradition. Sloan sat on a leather sofa, leaning back, his mind wandering. He couldn't stop thinking about Kendall, worrying about her, though he doubted she would appreciate his concern. And he was more apprehensive than he'd let on. Although he'd vigilantly studied the E.R. parking lot, he hadn't seen one thing, one person, that raised his radar.

But he felt a dark presence nearby. Hidden. Watching.

He feared the mercenaries who were now on Callahan land weren't newbies to the game. Unlike the last merc who'd tried to take his cousins down, whatever was here now was serious. Their grandfather had warned of three—which meant the enemy could gather a lot of intel while husbanding their resources and not stretching too thin.

Sloan's gut cramped. Kendall had been fortunate.

"I'll let Sloan fill you in on what happened," Jonas told the roomful of men and Ashlyn.

Sloan put down his crystal glass. "As you know, Fiona and our grandfather have decided we should stick together. I'm not sure about that," he said. "With the attack on Kendall, I feel pretty certain she was an intended kidnapping victim. I'll go with the general vote on whether we go undercover or remain on the ranch."

He knew everyone in the room had the same thing on their minds: How best to protect the whole family?

"We don't know what we're dealing with," Falcon said. "Kidnappings are a concern."

"Anything could happen—not to scare the hell out of you," Galen said.

Sloan saw his six Callahan cousins absorb this. They had families here. His side didn't have skin in the game—no children, no wives. They could pick up and leave tomorrow, and this would have just been a nice vacation for them.

Except Kendall. She needed a bodyguard, in his

opinion. She was tough, but a tiny woman like her was no match for a merc. The spirits had been on her side today.

The library doors opened. Chief Running Bear walked in, and everyone stood. Sam handed him a cut crystal tumbler of whiskey.

They all settled into the leather seats. Their grandfather set his glass on a table, his dark face serious. "Everything has changed."

Sloan cast a glance at his cousins. They were serious, alert. Listening.

The chief looked at all of them. "With this direct attack on the ranch, we must change the enemy's focus."

"What are you suggesting, Chief?" Jonas asked.

"Divide and conquer." The old man studied the people in the room, assessing their reaction to his words. He looked grave. "The situation is dangerous. The tactic must meet the moment. All Jeremiah's children and grandchildren must leave the ranch."

Sloan's cousins didn't say a word. He figured that had to be a huge bombshell dropped on them. But he also saw where the chief was going. With no one here, the mercs' purpose was essentially wasted. They were never going to find the Callahan parents; Molly and Jeremiah would never be given up by their sons.

Unless a child was kidnapped. All bets were off if children were involved in a ransom situation. And that was the utmost worry now on the chief's mind, Sloan felt certain, or his grandfather wouldn't have suggested such a radical tactic.

With sympathy, he met Jonas's gaze. But there was nothing Sloan could say. No one had expected the situation to get this dangerous so fast.

"Some can go to Dark Diablo. There's room there for

many," the chief said. "Others can go to Hell's Colony. Kendall and her brothers have offered their compound, which she says is large and safe. There's also transport for the children, and a staff to assist with the transition.

"I told her we were looking for a place for the children to go to school, for maybe the next half year. I didn't mention the mercenaries. When she's over the shock of what happened today, perhaps more can be explained. For now, she believes we're looking for a place where the children can also go to school. I was prepared to consider someplace in Canada, but Kendall has convinced me that, between the two locations, the family will be comfortable."

Sloan glanced around at his brothers and sister. Their grandfather's plan meant his family could all go back to their own homes. He would miss spending time with them. He'd thought they would be here longer, have more time together.

The chief looked directly at him. "You will stay here, Sloan, to keep an eye on the ranch. All of you, to watch over the Diablos, and the land."

They all glanced at each other, surprised.

"It's a lot of people to uproot," Sloan said, "much to change. The children's education, their friends." He didn't know why he was speaking up. The chief's plan was clear and concise, his preeminent goal to get the children and women out of the line of fire. Sloan got it—the plan was wise, strategic. Still, he understood how hard this would be on the families.

As a military operative, he'd lived alone for many years. Loneliness was part of the deal. But not for children.

"It's true," the chief said. "But there is no other way. There were no women, no children, before, but now there are many targets. I would not lose any of my family. Or my friends."

The chief meant Kendall. Sloan felt himself tense.

"Well," Jonas said, "there are two silver linings here. We have places to go, fortunately, because the Hilton would get expensive for as many of us as there are."

His brothers laughed, the tension lightening just a bit. There was, of course, no Hilton in Diablo, New Mexico.

"And thankfully, we have backup," he added, looking at Sloan.

After a long moment, Sloan nodded. For him, the mission had not changed all that much.

But it had become more personal than before.

KENDALL EYED SLOAN when he entered her room upstairs in the main house. "I have no makeup on," she said, "and I'm just vain enough that it matters. Plus I haven't showered. And I'm sulking because I'm stuck in here. So you've been warned." Her leg was atop a pillow, and she wore a tiny tank top and some heart-dotted shorts for comfort.

Sloan thought she looked sexy as hell.

He sat in the wingback chair next to the window. Not too close. "You got lucky."

"I guess." She winced, not wanting to dwell on the attack. "Anyway, just for the record, I knew you did something to put me to sleep. Don't do it again. I'm no fainting female who needs to be protected from the scary monsters."

He considered her. "You're very brave."

"It has nothing to do with bravery," Kendall said, "which is the part that scares me. I just reacted. But what if I'd frozen?"

She'd be dead or kidnapped. Sloan didn't mention that. Kendall would figure it out in time.

"So what was the meeting about? I heard a lot of footsteps on the stairs."

He thought her blond hair, which was pulled up into a ponytail, would probably be soft as a bird's wing if he ever got to touch it. "Jonas should probably be the one to tell you."

"You go ahead and tell me, soldier. My curiosity is killing me."

She was just the type of woman who would always want to have all the information. "Not my job, beautiful."

She stared at him. "Are you patronizing me?"

"Stating a fact. You are beautiful. The truth should not be an intimidating thing."

"Oh." She considered him for a moment. "That was pretty smooth for a guy who's supposed to be a loner."

He shrugged.

"Anyway, back to the subject matter," Kendall said. "What happened in the meeting?"

"I think," Sloan said, "change is in the wind."

"Because of what happened to me."

He inclined his head.

"Great." She sighed. "Sloan, I never got a good look at whatever it was. I feel kind of silly, if everybody's going to get upset about what happened, when it could have been…" She didn't know how to finish. It had been huge, and intending harm. New Mexico was fairly new to her, though she'd learned a lot about it in the year she'd worked for Jonas. "My mind keeps stupidly thinking bear, and yet I know it wasn't that. There are none around here."

"It was a human," Sloan said, "and the intent was to

take you, hold you for information. Your subconsciousness recognizes this."

Kendall blinked. "I don't have any information. Personal family stuff is never discussed with me."

"Ransom," Sloan offered. "Information for your freedom."

That made sense. She hated it, though, hated being party to someone—something—that threatened the Callahans. "So now what?"

"Everyone will move. Decamp to other places." He stood. "Can I get you a book? Cookies? Fiona is baking chocolate chip cookies, and I'm going to grab some on my way out."

She frowned at him. "What the hell does 'decamp' mean? You mean the whole family?"

"Right. To your compound, and to Dark Diablo. I believe my cousins have gone home to instruct their wives to pack up the children."

"Well, I did offer the compound to the chief when he told me he needed a vacation home for the clan," Kendall said, "but I didn't realize he meant no one would be *here*. That means me, too?"

He nodded. "Probably you especially."

"And you?" Her gaze met his.

"I'll likely sleep in your bed," Sloan teased, trying to get into her space just a little, to bedevil her, get her mind off the danger the Callahans—and her own family—were in.

And to get his mind off her, too.

"This bed." She sniffed. "If you like lace and flowers."

"I'll sleep very well."

A reluctant smile touched her lips. "Somehow I don't think you're a lace and flowers kind of guy."

He shrugged. "It isn't forever."

Could be forever. There was no way of knowing.

"Take care of yourself," he added.

"What does that mean? You sound like we're moving out immediately."

He went to the door. "You are. In the morning. The danger is here and you have to get away from it."

Sloan walked out, not wanting to think about how quiet the ranch would be without the children, without all the Callahans, and most of all, without the blonde who loved yanking his chain.

The fact that he might not see her very much—or ever again—after she left Rancho Diablo bothered him.

KENDALL ACCEPTED with a grateful smile the plate of cookies Fiona gave her. "You're an angel. Thank you so much. I really don't know what I would do without your cheery face right now." She hated to think that Fiona would be leaving the ranch. Fiona and Burke were the heart of Rancho Diablo, in Kendall's mind. They were always there, to comfort, to give a warm word of wisdom, perhaps just an encouraging smile. "Are you going to Dark Diablo or our house in Hell's Colony?"

"I'm staying right here." Fiona sat in the same wingback chair Sloan had been sitting in not forty minutes ago. "Burke and I have too much work to do."

"Did you tell Jonas?"

Fiona nodded, sipped her cup of hot tea. "He's not happy. But I'm the aunt. I get to do what I want at my age. Anyway, I'm in no danger." She smiled at Kendall. "How's the leg?"

"Sore. But not as sore as my ego." Kendall wouldn't admit the feeling of helplessness she had from the attack. It was almost as if part of her confidence had been stolen. Her soul.

Fiona nodded. "Perfectly normal. Takes a while to pass."

"I'm not a good victim. Especially when I don't know what it was." Kendall considered Fiona. The wiry Callahan aunt sat smiling, as if nothing was wrong. But she had to be worried sick. "You're trying to keep my mind off what's going on."

Fiona shrugged. "Seems to me we can't do anything but wait."

"I don't wait well."

"Neither do I. Still, you'll heal. Your leg, your heart." Fiona set her teacup in its saucer on the tiny side table. "Where will you go?"

Sloan would be here. There'd be plenty of Callahans on the premises. And Fiona and Burke. "I'm staying right here. I can work from my room. No one will come into this house. I'm safe as a princess in an ivory tower. And you need another female on the ranch to talk to."

Fiona stood. "Good luck telling Jonas. He'll read you the riot act and tell you that as his employee, you have to go. That your insurance is too high to run such a risk. And that he wants you directing the traffic flow of tiny bodies at your compound."

Kendall smiled. "There's an army of people at Hell's Colony who will be delighted to have small feet running around." In fact, it just might bring her mother and new husband home from the perpetual honeymoon they'd been on, leaving Kendall, Xav, Shaman and Gage to manage the compound and Gil Phillips, Inc.

"You know, Fiona, our business is moving large equipment in our cargo planes. Worldwide. If we ever needed to, we could always take the family out of the country, if this goes on for a while."

She nodded. "I pray the day never comes. Surely the danger is just here at this ranch."

Who knew what they were dealing with? Kendall certainly didn't. "Is Sloan still downstairs?"

"Last I saw." Fiona got up, carrying her teacup with her. "Do you need to talk to him?"

Kendall nodded. "Yes, thank you. If you don't mind asking him to come back up for just a minute."

"I'll see you in the morning. Feel better!" She smiled at Kendall. "I don't mind telling you that I'll be glad to have another female on the ranch."

"I suppose Ashlyn will be around somewhere," Kendall said.

"I don't know. We all do what the chief tells us. Well, everyone but you and me." Laughing, Fiona left.

A moment later, Kendall heard Sloan's footsteps on the landing. He poked his head into the room.

She frowned. "Come in, please. Shut the door."

He did, and perched on the arm of the chair. "Talk, Blondie."

"My name is Kendall. Not Barbie, not Blondie."

"Gotcha." He smiled, slow and dangerous, a reminder that she didn't really know this man she was about to give all of her trust.

Kendall knew that, but she'd never run from a fight. "Sloan, after all the Callahans leave in the morning, I want you to take me somewhere."

"Anywhere. Name it."

"The spot near the canyon, where the new bunkhouse will be."

He gave her a long look. "You don't have to face it so soon. Give yourself some time."

"I've lived a long time without you advising me. Either you take me or I'll go by myself."

"You can't drive with those stitches."

"Let me tell you something about me that you don't know. I would bounce on one of the Callahan kids' pogo sticks to get back there if I have to. It's my job, and I will do it."

"Whatever you say."

"Jonas won't like it."

"It's all right. I'll play chauffeur. You rest."

She closed her eyes, suddenly tired. "Thank you."

She felt him near her bed, felt him peek at the bandage covering her stitches, run a palm over her calf, testing for changes in her skin temperature.

"Don't you dare pull any of that mumbo-jumbo stuff on me again," Kendall said. "I'm going to read a book, and I don't want to go to sleep. I'm still teed off with you."

He sat on the edge of her bed, the mattress dipping under his weight. She wished she could open her eyes to glare at him, but she was just so darn tired.

"Rest," he said, and she said, "You're annoying. Has anyone ever told you that?"

But when Sloan touched his palm to her cheek, she relaxed against his hand, drawing in his strength.

It felt good to have someone take care of her just for a moment. Not Kendall against the world… Right now, she let Sloan chase the unspoken fear away.

Tomorrow I'll be strong again.

Chapter Five

Close, close. The wolf was so close, its eyes fierce with anger and malice. It wanted his soul, wanted his lifeblood. Sloan jerked awake, his heart thundering.

He cursed under his breath when he realized he'd fallen asleep in Kendall's bed, against the headboard, her head against his chest, her long blond ponytail trailing to his abdomen.

This was bad. In the military, snipers didn't allow emotions to get in the way of the job.

His emotions were definitely becoming involved. He had to stop it from happening.

Carefully, he disengaged himself from Kendall, laying her slowly back in her bed. God, she was soft. So feminine. She acted so brave, but what had happened had wounded her, revealing the vulnerability she hid so well.

He went downstairs, knowing he had to make sure—damn sure—his unfortunate lapse didn't endanger his senses, his assignment, or her.

"Hey." Jonas filled up a coffee mug, slid it his way. "Let's talk, cousin."

Sloan followed him into a large den filled with dark brown leather furniture and a huge TV. Toys were stacked in a playpen in the corner. Clearly, this room was one of the children's hangouts, no doubt because of its proximity to Fiona's kitchen. Jonas put a tray stacked with his aunt's fresh-baked cookies on the coffee table in front of them. Sloan perched on a chair, wanting a direct face-to-face with his cousin.

"We pull out at 0500. Cover of darkness is essential," Jonas said. "We hope that whoever might be spying on the ranch won't see us leave."

"Good idea."

"We'll be using a series of vehicles. There'll be too many of us to follow, if they should see us leave. As the chief said, divide and conquer."

"Wise strategy." Sloan nodded.

"Some of us will pass around Diablo, double back here. Rafe has the jet ready. Some of the children and wives will travel on it to Hell's Colony. The vehicles we plan to leave in town. I'm asking you to get them back here when you can."

"No problem."

"I'll show you the firearms we have on the ranch. The chief knows where everything else is. Money. Whatever."

Sloan blinked. "We won't need money."

"Someone has to run the ranch."

"Fiona will be here. And Kendall is your employee, right?"

Jonas nodded. "But we all agree we'd feel better with a Callahan heir handling ranch transactions. I don't mean grocery store bills and things that affect the household—Fiona and Burke have been doing that for years. I'm talking about whatever needs to be done to make certain this ranch is kept secure."

"I understand." Jonas wanted them to have whatever they needed to protect the houses, livestock and the wild Diablo mustangs.

"There's a cache of silver in the basement. It has a specific purpose." Jonas looked at him. "You can get the rest of the info on that from the chief. That's just between you and me, cousin."

Sloan nodded again.

Jonas gave him a hard stare. "I also charge you with convincing Kendall to eventually come to Hell's Colony. I know she won't leave the ranch now, but that was the drugs talking. It's important that she not be here. She could have been taken, or worse. It's not safe for her."

"I'll do my best."

"If you have to hypnotize her again, do it."

Sloan shook his head. "She asked me not to. Actually," he said, "she didn't ask me. It was more like she commanded me never to do it again." The memory of her ragging him about it made him smile. She refused to admit that she'd been in shock and pain, and relaxing helped. He admired the fact that she would choose pain over giving up any independence. "I can't do it. She's not a willing subject."

"She's not a willing subject about anything. Why do I always have stubborn women around me?" Jonas asked. But the question was rhetorical, Sloan knew. Jonas was crazy about Fiona, about his wife, Sabrina, who was rumored to have a very stubborn streak, and even Kendall.

"Strong men draw strong women," Sloan said.

"Lovely. Just once I'd like to have a 'Yes, Jonas' type of female in my life." He got up to pace, so Sloan reached for a cookie, biting into it with pleasure. The simple pleasure of a home-baked cookie was something he hadn't had in years. Not since—

"Sloan."

"Yes." He straightened, focusing on Jonas again. "I'm listening."

"Whatever you do, you can't let Kendall run you around."

Sloan hesitated. "Meaning?"

"She's bossy. She thinks she can handle herself. And handle anything. The truth is, she doesn't really know much about what's been happening here over the past four years. She doesn't know much about the family." Jonas paced some more, his body darkly silhouetted in front of the huge window where the moon shone into the den, touching the furnishings with dim light. "She knows a little, but not enough to convince herself she can't go about her duties the way she used to. I know Kendall. She'll decide she imagined the whole thing, that she hurt herself on the jeep. Like maybe a big bird flew over and startled her or something. The next thing you know, she'll be back out there, making plans for the new bunkhouse."

Sloan swallowed. "I'll get her out to Hell's Colony somehow." It would be for the best.

He looked at Jonas. "I think I have an answer to your problem."

"I would love to hear it," Jonas replied, appearing relieved. "Please share."

"Fire her," Sloan said.

Jonas looked stunned. Then he laughed. "That's perfect."

Sloan felt bad, but saving Kendall from Kendall was paramount.

"Wish I'd thought of it." He got up, slapped Sloan

on the back. "I'll leave you to take care of that tomorrow morning, after we're gone, cousin."

Jonas walked out. Sloan grimaced, the delicious cookie no longer appealing.

It was going to be a long night. The dream wolf had long been his nocturnal companion, a shadowy fear that kept peace at bay and shredded his sleep.

But he'd rather face the wolf than the woman who was going to be none too happy when he told her that her services were no longer required.

"WHAT?" Kendall exclaimed in a shriek. She glared at Sloan. "What do you mean, I'm *fired?*"

Damn Jonas for leaving this mission to him. Sloan leaned against the wall in Kendall's room and shrugged—although the last thing he felt was calm and uncaring.

"Fired. Out of work."

Her blue eyes narrowed on him. "You did this."

He sighed. "I did."

Kendall threw the nearest thing that could be used as a projectile, which happened to be her hairbrush, since he'd caught her in the middle of trying to fix herself for the day. The brush bounced off the wall, not one inch from his face. "I'll have you know my services command hundreds of thousands of dollars. If I call up any of the corporations who've tried to lure me away from Gil Phillips, Inc., in the past year, I'll have a position in thirty minutes, and a salary that would make your head swim."

He nodded. "Your right to do so."

She shot a heart-decorated flip-flop at him, followed by its mate. They both missed, but she was getting warmed up, and Sloan figured the next time she'd peg him.

"Get out."

"I'm under orders to get you to Hell's Colony."

"Orders? I've been *fired. I* don't take orders from Jonas Callahan anymore, that supercilious ass." She hopped out of the bed, her face creasing with pain as she tried to stay off her foot. "And you promised to take me out to the canyons, though I see now you're not a man of your word."

She hobbled to the landing. "Jonas!" she yelled down the stairwell.

"He's gone. They're all gone."

She hopped back into the room, staring at him. "What do you mean, they're all gone?"

"There's no one on the ranch but my family, and Fiona and Burke."

"Oh, my God." She sank onto her bed again, and Sloan felt sympathy for her. He knew how it felt to lose everything. "I didn't know they'd leave this soon. No wonder it's so quiet. I thought the children were all watching a movie in the bunkhouse or something."

He shook his head. "They left before the sun was up this morning."

"I can't believe it. And yet I'm relieved." She gazed at Sloan. "And you're supposed to fire me so I'll leave, too."

"Yeah." He nodded. "Jonas was too chicken to do it."

"I'll bet." Kendall sat silently for a moment. "You're both chickenhearted weasels. But at least you told me to my face."

"I'm a gentleman."

"Whatever." Kendall didn't look at him. "I'm not leaving."

Sloan's heart sank. He should have seen this coming. No wonder Jonas had gone off like a dog not eager to see a bathtub. Swallowing hard, Sloan stared at Kendall, reading her face. She was thinking, thinking hard—and he was in trouble.

"*You* hire me," Kendall said.

"What?" He blinked, automatically stiffening.

"You're in charge here now. You hire me." Kendall raised a brow, challenging him.

"I can't do that." Sloan shook his head. "I have no authority to make hiring decisions."

"This is a combat zone. You can make decisions without Jonas's okay." Her determined expression said she wasn't about to let this go. "Besides which, you want me here."

His gaze snapped to hers. "I don't—"

"Yes, you do." She crossed her arms. "You'd feel a whole lot better if you could keep your eyes on me."

His eyes and some other things. Sloan resisted his errant thoughts. "No can do, sweetheart. Be a good girl and mind your ex-boss. He knows what's best for you. Me, I'm just an interloper."

"You're a tough guy," Kendall said. "And tough guys like to do things themselves. You want to protect me, don't you?"

He wasn't falling for the boost to his ego. "You'll be safe in Texas. Where you belong." He got up, went to the door. "I'll have one of my brothers take you to Albuquerque so you can catch a plane."

"Sloan."

He wished he didn't have to stay in here with her any longer. She was winding tendrils of temptation around him, and the worst part was, he knew she was doing it. Didn't really want to stop it. "Yeah?"

"I'm staying. I'm going to stick it out with Fiona and Burke. This may not be my home, but I'm not giving up the job I've already put several months of work into planning. And you wouldn't, either, if you were me."

His mouth flattened. "You have to leave. All the rest of it I'm not getting drawn into."

He walked out, feeling a ball of tension knot his neck. Everything she'd said was true: he did want her here. He did think he could do the best job of protecting her. But she'd be safe in Texas, where Jonas said her family had a compound.

The problem was, Kendall knew he'd thought up the plan to fire her, so she knew Jonas still wanted her to finish his bunkhouse—when the danger passed. She didn't consider herself to be in danger, so she saw no reason not to go on with her whatever-the-hell-it-was that she did. Decorating or something. She was fiery like his sister, Ashlyn, and Sloan had plenty of experience with that.

So he knew what the next step was.

"Ashlyn, go upstairs and keep an eye on Kendall for a while, please." He walked past his sister, who'd stationed herself in the kitchen near Fiona and Burke, who seemed pretty content to ignore everything that didn't have anything to do with baking and cooking. "Don't let her talk you into anything. She'll probably try."

"Sure." Ashlyn slid off the barstool and left the kitchen.

Fiona glanced his way. "Problems?"

Sloan took the sack she handed him, which he assumed contained a lunch. "No problems. Thank you for this."

She nodded and he left, not one bit happy with the

blonde upstairs. She was right: he didn't want her to leave.

But she was going to, whether he liked it or not.

She didn't understand about the wolf.

Chapter Six

At ten o'clock that night, Sloan took over from Ashlyn.

"I've got it, Ash. Thanks." He slumped into the wingback chair, a semiautomatic tucked into a holster under his arm, hidden from Kendall. The gun was to level the playing field in case they were attacked—though it seemed too soon for the enemy to make a move. They'd be trying to figure out where everyone had gone, and who was left here, and why.

"You're back," Kendall said, opening her eyes to glare at him. "I prefer your sister babysitting me."

He nodded. "Everyone prefers Ashlyn. Now be a good girl and let me sleep."

She sat up. "I don't like your tone, soldier."

"That's a shame." He lowered his hat over his face. Maybe she'd take the hint that it was time for lights out.

"It's condescending. Smacks of arrogance. Like you think you're in charge of everything."

"I am." No further comment needed to be made.

"Bully for you. I'm going to take a shower."

His eyes widened under his dark gray Stetson. He refused to let his mind wander in the direction it wanted very much to go. There was a bath en suite, so she couldn't escape him—but on the other hand, he couldn't escape her, either.

He stayed under his hat, although he couldn't have slept now if he wanted to.

She hummed quietly. He heard her pulling out drawers, choosing clothes.

"Can't forget the panties," Kendall said, and Sloan gritted his teeth. "Although since I'm on bed rest one more day, a bra isn't essential, I suppose."

She was torturing him on purpose.

"Thankfully, I have this leg wrap the hospital gave me to keep the stitches dry," Kendall said conversationally, as if she wasn't trying to drive him mad. She lifted the brim of his hat, peeking at him. "Comfy?"

Not really. "I will be when you quit chattering."

She smiled, her blue gaze sweet. "I'll call you if I need anything."

He swallowed, pinned. She dropped his hat back on his head and went humming into the bathroom. The water turned on, and he imagined her dropping her pajama shorts and camisole to the floor. Warmth broke out under his hat, lining his hatband with a trace of sweat.

He turned his focus inside, concentrating on the beat of his heart, the rhythm of his pulse, commanding himself to calm down.

After a moment, the wild feeling passed. He wasn't attracted to Kendall—not at all—so there had been no reason for the surge of panic. Feeling better now that he was in control of the situation, Sloan leaned back, propping his head against the chair back, and tried to doze.

Kendall began singing a catchy tune, and the scent of strawberry shampoo drifted out to him. He pushed his hat back from his forehead, needing air. The chair was positioned directly across from the bath, so he was right in the line of fire.

There was a reason she was trying to get under his skin, and it had to do with control. But it wasn't going to work. His self-control was steel forged by fire.

"Sloan?"

He hesitated. Went to the bathroom door. "Yeah?"

"I forgot a towel."

That was as old as the trees. He wasn't falling for it. "Drip dry."

She laughed. "I can't. I have to dry the plastic sleeve that covers my stitches. I can't get them wet. My towel is on my bed."

It was a trap, it had to be. He'd simply open the door and fling the stupid thing onto the counter. She'd have to take it from there.

He grabbed the towel and opened the door, ready to make the toss onto the granite-topped counter. But he caught a glimpse of Kendall in the shower, silhouetted through the frosted glass, her head back as she rinsed her hair, still humming that dumb song. He could see breasts outlined through the glass, and her hair falling back in a sleek sweep, nearly reaching her sexy rounded buttocks.

He threw the towel, slammed the door and staggered to the chair, falling into it with a smothered curse.

She was a goddess. That much beauty was enough to kill a lesser man. He was stuck protecting it.

It wasn't going to kill him. He was simply going to control his mind so that he didn't think about the beautifully rounded breasts or the—

He breathed, began the technique of self-hypnosis that never failed him. He had this.

This was his job, and he'd always been a loyal soldier. He'd always done his job.

This time would be no different.

KENDALL CAME OUT OF the bathroom feeling like a new woman. She slipped into her bed, happily pulling the sheet up to her neck—but then she realized Sloan was sound asleep, his head tilted at an awkward angle in the wingback chair.

"Hey! Tough guy."

He didn't move.

Okay, he was going to have a helluva crick in his neck in the morning. "Although why I should care, I don't know, you annoying Callahan." She grabbed the small, fringed, tubular-shaped lumbar pillow off the bed and went over to Sloan, trying to figure out how to stick it behind his neck without waking him. He seemed to be deep in sleep, so the maneuver should be easy enough. And anyway, she didn't care if she did wake him up. It would serve him right for being such a horse's rear. She jammed the pillow under his neck, springing back a bit when he moved, opened one sleepy eye—before both eyes came open to glare at her.

"What are you doing?"

"Oh, my goodness," Kendall said, exasperated. "Trying to smother you with a lacy pillow, you freak. What does it look like?"

His gaze moved from her face to her throat, then slid down to her breasts, which he could probably see through the white cami top. His eyes shot back to hers. "Thanks."

"You're welcome. You didn't look comfortable."

He watched as she got back into bed, his gaze hard

on her as she pulled the sheet snugly up to her neck. "I don't need a pillow."

"I know." Kendall sighed. "You're a hard case. You sleep on rocks and you eat rocks and you drink water you smite from rock. Go back to sleep."

She flounced over onto her side, thoroughly put out with him.

"Sleeping on rocks or wood is not all that uncommon in some civilizations," Sloan said.

"That's nice. Just sit over there and enjoy the crick in your neck. I'm going to doze off on these wonderful feather pillows." Kendall blinked, struck by a random thought. "Have you ever slept on a feather pillow?"

He laughed. "Sure. Every night. The military gives them out like candy. Every good grunt carries one."

She tossed one of her pillows at him, catching him in the face. "Try it. You might like it. And if you get a good night's sleep, maybe you won't be such a crab tomorrow."

"I'm a crab," Sloan said, "because you won't follow orders."

She sat up. "Whose orders? Your orders? Jonas's orders?" Jumping up, she jerked the pillow away from him and got back into bed. "I'm not leaving! Whoever is here—and I'm assuming you Callahans think someone is here or the families wouldn't have left—they're not after me, because I don't know anything. I'm the safest of all, especially with you and all your siblings prowling around the place. I'm not going to abandon my friends, with whom I've been employed for some years and lived with often, just because you thought it was a great idea to fire me. But I don't think you can understand the concept of loyalty. Because all you know is how to follow orders." She gave Sloan a look of disgust. "I'm not a soldier. I've never followed orders a day in my life."

"Tell me something I couldn't figure out on my own." Sloan's tone was dry. He sounded as if he might even have a smile in his voice, which irritated her to no end.

"If anyone is in danger, it would be Fiona. She's the keeper of the family history, and if there's a reason to kidnap someone and hold them for information, don't you think an elderly woman would be a prime target?"

Sloan looked at Kendall for a long moment. "I'll be right back."

"That's what I thought," she muttered, then turned back over, resting her cheek on the soft pillow. She made certain her leg was propped up, and then closed her eyes and released a long breath.

Now that the reason for all her frustration had left the room, she could finally relax. He was so full of himself, such an arrogant guy—and so handsome he made her nervous.

The thing was, she didn't think she'd ever been so hot for a man in all her life. Which was just the way things went: the one guy her body responded to in years, and he had to be the one she couldn't have. Anything between them was such an illogical fantasy that she couldn't even understand her attraction to him. But the attraction was real, and mystifying. They didn't even get along.

Yet he'd seemed pretty appreciative of her putting the pillow behind his neck, after he'd gotten used to the idea of someone worrying about his comfort. And he was committed to the idea of sleeping in that stupid chair, although it wasn't made for long-term sitting or resting.

Maybe he was a tad more heroic than she wanted to admit. Sort of a rough hero. She'd never had a hero in her life before, besides her brothers, so the experience was new.

And unfortunately, insanely hot.

SLOAN RETURNED an hour later, after assigning Falcon to watch over Fiona and Burke for the night, to find Kendall sitting on the edge of the bed, her eyes wide as she stared out the window.

"What is it?"

"I thought I saw something." She turned a panicked gaze toward him.

He went to the window, peering out, careful not to reveal himself to anyone who might be scoping out the house. "There's a lot of people here. My family, some workers." He turned to her. "What do you think you saw?"

"A man. A big man." Kendall's eyes widened. "Tall, thin, hiding behind the bunkhouse before he walked toward the barns."

She might have seen something. Then again, perhaps she didn't know all the workers on the grounds. But it was just as likely that she did; Jonas said Kendall had been working at his two properties for the past year, along with her brothers. They'd moved their own base of operations to the ranches, flying wherever they needed to meet clients and liaisons. "No one can get in the house. Falcon is standing guard. My brothers and Ash are around. The workers have been posted to let us know if they see anything suspicious. Try to sleep."

She moved stiffly toward the white lace pillows. "I'm not as brave as you think I am."

"Yeah, you are." He settled into the wingback chair.

"You've had a shock. It's just now hitting you. Maybe some hot tea would be calming."

She shook her head. "I don't want to stay awake."

"I'm right here. No one's coming through that door." He put his gun on the tiny table. "You're safe."

"Okay."

She lay down, her body rigid and stiff under the covers. He could see her tension, knew that nerves had finally hit her, and awareness was cutting into the bravado she'd been shielding herself with.

He moved the chair closer to her bed, pulled off his boots and put his feet up on the end.

"Thank you for being here," she said, her voice small.

"Go to sleep. Or I'll have to hypnotize you," he teased.

"I can't. I know you're not comfortable, and it's making me worry. Stretch out here beside me so I can sleep." Kendall put two king-size ruffled pillows down the center of the bed. "There's your wall of fire."

He sighed. "Barbie, a wall of fire like that wouldn't stop a horny male. I'll stay over here."

She looked his way. "Why? Are you…horny?"

"God, no." He was bone-tired. "I'm just saying your pillow wall wouldn't exactly be recommended in terms of security."

"I'm assuming you have some sense of chivalry, as well."

"I don't." He closed his eyes.

"Then get up on the bed, on top of the covers, so I can sleep. You can practice chivalry and I'll stop shaking."

"Are you shaking?" That concerned him. "Okay, I'll lie down. Don't touch me, Barbie."

"Believe me, I'd rather gnaw off my pink vinyl arm. Stop calling me that, you chauvinist."

"All right. Now close your pink vinyl lips. A guy doesn't get much sleep around you needy types."

"That's right," Kendall said. "Blame the woman."

He grinned in the dark. Then he smelled strawberry shampoo as he settled onto the feather pillow, and quit smiling. She was so near, tantalizingly close.

He wasn't going to get a single minute of sleep.

But if she did, it would be worth it.

SLOAN AWAKENED in the night, his eyes wide-open. An arm had curved around his waist as someone snuggled up to his back. Warm, rounded breasts pressed against his shoulder blades.

Kendall.

Her cheek rested near his neck. He closed his eyes, for a moment indulging in her warmth and the sexiness of her body pushed up against his. "Kendall. Damn it. Get back on your side of the pillows."

"Oh. Sorry." She kind of giggled in her sleep, and rolled over.

Sloan drew in a deep breath. Now they were both saved from embarrassment in the morning.

Yeah, you're a hero. Dummy.

She'd felt wonderful curled up against him. He'd never experienced anything that glorious in his entire life. His skin practically erupted in goose bumps at the memory of her breasts against him.

"I'm trying to protect you," he told her, not sure if she'd drifted back to sleep.

"I know, you goof. Quit trying to be such an angel. It's a little cold in this room, you're warm and I accidentally got into your space. I'm not apologizing. I'll go to Hell's Colony tomorrow, so you don't have to be so worried, okay? Now pipe down. I thought you were the loner in the family, and I swear you're as chatty as Dolly Parton in *Nine To Five.*"

He'd seen that movie on one of the bases he'd been stationed at, though he couldn't remember which one. His mouth twisted. She had no idea what kind of man was sleeping in her bed. He was as dangerous as the mercenaries that were after the Callahans—he just happened to be working on the good side. "I'm just trying to spare you any awkwardness—"

"Blah, blah, blah, blah, blah," Kendall said, her voice sleepy. "I'm sorry I invaded your zone, soldier. You're doing a great job. Sign off and go back to your post."

He wryly grinned, rolling over onto his side. She had no idea how much strength it took not to violate the terms of his engagement here. After he heard her breathing return to a gentle, sonorous rhythm, he got out of bed to look outside.

She was right about it being colder. A thick layer of snow had fallen, casting a white blanket over the roofs of the barns and bunkhouse. Glancing at his phone, he saw that the temperature had dropped to twelve degrees Fahrenheit.

That meant two things: one, he didn't need to keep his promise to take her to photograph the canyons today. She was stuck inside where she'd be safe. Two, she wouldn't be flying or driving out today. He checked the forecast, seeing that the snow should continue for the next week.

He doubted very seriously that Kendall was the kind of woman who stayed cooped up very well. It was three o'clock in the morning, and snowflakes continued to drift down in big, wet, thick abundance. Maybe he should toss another blanket on top of her for warmth.

Pile another layer of security between them.

A dark shadow on the snow caught his eye. It was just a random pattern in the white light from the spotlights shining from the bunkhouse, but still he waited at the window, frowning.

He texted Tighe, who was stationed as lookout at the bunkhouse. Watch your door.

The reply came back swiftly. On it.

Sloan texted Jace. Back up Tighe.

Again, swift reply. Got it.

Barely two seconds passed before he saw his brothers checking out something in the deep snow. He waited, watching for a signal.

We've got company, Tighe wrote.

Sloan sent a mass text to his brothers. Man on-site.

"What is it?" Kendall asked, sitting up.

Damn it. "Nothing. Go back to sleep."

She crossed to the window to see what he was staring at. He tried to shove her back. Taking exception, Kendall popped him a good one on the shoulder, knocking him slightly off balance because he hadn't expected her to be so strong.

"What are they doing?"

"What they're supposed to do." Standing beside her, he returned his gaze to his brothers, watching closely for danger, his semi in his hand. Sloan got ready to jack open the window and fire if necessary—vaguely aware of the scent of strawberries invading his usual tight self-control.

Chapter Seven

Kendall stared down at the Callahans—and of course her brother, Xav, was in the thick of it—stunned as they grabbed a man from a deep snowdrift and wrestled him into the bunkhouse. The door closed, and it was like watching someone get sucked into another dimension. No sound, too fast for struggle—it was simply over.

"What was *that?*" Kendall demanded. "What just happened?"

"Back in bed, gorgeous," Sloan told her. "I don't do your job, you don't do mine."

She smacked at his hands as he tried to shoo her away from the window. "Tell me what is going on, Sloan, or I'll go out there myself."

"Not dressed like that. You'll give the watchmen heart attacks."

She snatched up a blanket, wrapping it around herself. "I'm going to check on Fiona and Burke."

"They're fine. Stay here."

She whirled on her way to the door. "Your brothers just abducted somebody. And what about my brother? Why don't you want me to check on Fiona and Burke?"

"They've got more protection than you do." Sloan eased into the chair. "I just got six texts saying everything is under control. What we don't need is you running around in your underwear with a gimp leg, trying to protect the old folks. Go back to sleep. I have to be up in an hour and a half." He checked his gun, made sure the lock was back on, and put it into the holster.

Now he had to figure out how he was going to calm the wild-eyed blonde glaring at him.

"I want you to check on Fiona and Burke."

"I have." He held up his phone. "Galen says the house is secure. Was never breached."

"Then what happened?"

"I don't know yet. I can't do my job because I have a hysterical female to soothe."

"I don't find you remotely soothing, thanks. And I've never been hysterical in my life."

"Get in bed. I'll bring you a cup of hot tea."

She glanced toward the window. "I don't need tea. I don't need you."

That was fear talking. Maybe Kendall didn't even recognize it herself. She was going to have to get over it. "Okay," he said, his voice soft. "I'm going to go out for a while."

She stared at him, her eyes huge like an animal desperate not to get preyed upon. "A while?"

"Yeah."

She glanced nervously at the window, then back to him. Got into bed. For a moment he thought he'd made her realize she was safest here.

"I'll go with you."

She jumped out of bed, long limbs in motion, and began pulling a sweatshirt over her cami, stretching the thin material to accommodate her breasts. A lump formed in his throat.

"You can't go with me."

She snorted. "I'm going. Figure out a way to brace yourself, because it's happening."

Big-time backfire on his plan. "You can go as far as the kitchen, make us both a cup of tea and grab us some cookies or something. I'll check with my brothers and see what they caught. Then you meet me back upstairs, and I'll tell you everything I find out. Can we compromise on that?"

She pulled on some comfy pajama bottoms that wouldn't abrade her stitches. "Sure, soldier. I can obey orders when I'm not being patronized."

He wouldn't bet on her being a good follower. But determination was all over her face, so this time it was probably better to give in. "Stay close to me."

"That's a harder order to obey."

"You got pretty close to me in bed last night. Didn't seem too hard on you."

She didn't say anything as they went down the stairwell, but she did get right up close to him.

A hand fell across Sloan's back. He heard a muffled squeal from Kendall.

"Falcon."

His brother appeared from the shadows. "Fiona and Burke haven't moved. Slept like babies."

"Oh, thank heaven," Kendall said.

"I told you the house was never breached," Sloan said, his voice quiet.

"Like I trust you to tell me the truth!" Kendall slipped past him. "I'm going to make tea. You want some, Falcon?"

"Sure." He grinned at Sloan. "My job's easier than yours."

"I heard that, Falcon," Kendall said. "Would you like some arsenic with your tea?"

The brothers rolled their eyes at each other and shrugged. Sloan heard Kendall put the kettle on. She didn't turn on a light in the kitchen, clearly deciding that the cover of darkness was necessary.

"I'm going out," Falcon said.

"I'm coming, too." Sloan followed his brother.

"What about her?"

"She'll be fine. We're just going to the bunkhouse, Kendall," he called.

"Okay."

She sounded a bit more nervous than he would have expected her to. Sloan glanced back, to find her staring down at the mugs she'd set out, not moving.

Well, this was as good a time as any for her to figure out whether she wanted him to be her bodyguard. She was here until the roads could be traveled, so they were stuck together.

He went out the door.

IT WAS REALLY COLD. Or maybe she was just shivering from whatever had happened out there. Kendall picked up her mug and went to the window. Nothing was revealed in the darkness. Even footprints had been covered over by the fast-falling snowflakes.

Sloan appeared from the bunkhouse, crunched through the snow to the main house and came inside in a swirling burst of frigid air. Kendall handed him a steaming mug of tea.

"What happened?"

His cold fingers touched hers for a split second as he gratefully took the hot drink. "The good news is that it wasn't a merc."

She wasn't sure he wasn't just trying to calm her down. "Do I believe you?"

He drank some of the tea. "That's good. Thanks. I'm going to bed. If I hurry, I have thirty minutes before I need to head to the barns. And no, it's not always good to believe me. I didn't sign an honesty clause. I said I'd protect you."

She followed him up the stairs. "What's the point of not being honest?"

"In this case, I am. I'm just saying in general it's okay if you don't trust me. You don't know me."

He pulled off his shirt in the dimness, not bothering to turn on the light. The spotlights shone outside the window, but otherwise it was deathly dark and quiet, thanks to the snowfall. He had a broad chest and wonderful pecs, a lean waist and—

"Let me take that. I'll hang it in the bathroom."

"Thanks." He handed her the shirt and shucked off his jeans.

Kendall's breath caught. She didn't bother to try to turn her eyes away, though she probably should.

He wore black briefs that molded to his hips—and he had great legs. Did guys have "great legs"? It didn't matter. Sloan did. In fact, he was pretty much the most attractive male she'd ever laid eyes on.

She put out a hand for the jeans.

"These are wet. They'll have to go in the dryer," Sloan said.

"I know." She took the clothes, draped them over a rack in the bathroom, noticing that the warmth of his body still clung to them though he'd been out in the cold. After taking a moment to try to think about what she wanted, what was right, Kendall went back into the bedroom.

He'd slid into the bed, underneath the sheets and

blankets. The wall of king-size pillows was firmly in place.

After a long pause, she got into bed. Sloan's breathing was deep, even. She thought about the forbidden aspect of mingling business with pleasure.

To him, she was business.

She'd always taken care of herself.

Taking a deep breath, she moved the pillows away. And curled up against his wide, muscular back.

SLOAN DIDN'T FALL ASLEEP while Kendall was in the lavatory; he was wide-awake, tense. He hadn't been completely honest with her about the man they'd intercepted. The intruder wasn't a contract killer—but he'd been sent to scout information about the Callahans and relay whatever he learned back to his employers.

Sloan's brothers had not quite drawn all the information from the scout—but they would. As much as the man actually knew, anyway. Sloan doubted the team of mercenaries who'd hired the nearly illiterate man had told him much. His brothers would get out what they could.

Sloan saw no reason to share any of this with Kendall. He heard her moving around in the bathroom, situating his clothes, and thought about what might have happened to her if she hadn't been so fast, so courageous, when she'd been attacked. Her sense of independence had already been shaken. She didn't need to know any more about the scout.

She needed to leave the ranch, though. Sloan had to convince her.

She came out of the bath, and the scent of strawberry wafted to him. He felt her get into bed, lift the covers and settle in. He let out a breath—then tensed up hard when the pillows moved. The movement was deliberate, and he couldn't miss the message when she curled up against his back, laying her cheek between his shoulder blades.

Sloan squeezed his eyes shut. "What's up, baby girl?"

She ran a hand up his chest, holding him to her. "Make love to me, Sloan."

He swallowed hard. "You've had a shock, Kendall. It's normal to reach out. But that's not what you really want."

"Glad to hear I'm normal." Her forehead pressed against his back; he could feel her slight breath against his skin. Ripples of desire ran through him. He deserved a medal for withstanding this onslaught of female invitation. She slipped her hand down his abs, flattening her palm above his groin. "But I don't need a psychological evaluation. I need you."

He was only so much of a saint. In fact, he wasn't a saint at all. Sloan rolled over, crushing her beneath him. He took her hand, shoved it up above her head so that he pinned her. "Kendall, tomorrow you'll feel differently. Tonight you're scared. I understand that. But I'm not the answer."

"I'm not looking for answers." She moved his hand off her wrist and ran her palms up his back, pressing him closer. "You treat me like a china doll. As if you're afraid of me."

"I'm not…" Kendall did scare the hell out of him. They had nothing in common except Rancho Diablo, which wasn't even his home, nor hers.

The problem was how much he wanted her.

Chapter Eight

It wasn't easy throwing herself out on the edge. Kendall knew Sloan would probably have some kind of alpha-male fit all over her for trying to seduce him. He treated her like she was too fragile to have human emotions. She did—and right now, she was giving in to them.

"I want you, Sloan."

He didn't reply. He'd tensed up, practically a hard stone fortress in her arms—but then his lips touched hers, seeking, before turning demanding.

Sparks ignited inside her. She kissed him back, drawing him to her, not about to let him get up on his good-soldier horse and ride away. Moving her hips beneath his, she teased and mocked his self-control, daring him to turn away from her.

He groaned, and the teasing turned to urgency. Sloan kissed her like a dying man, his touch stroking, invading, loving.

Kendall thought she would scream if he didn't let go of his iron self-control. He was hard and muscular in her arms, his lips everywhere—and at the moment she thought she was going to die if she didn't get him inside her. But then Sloan slid her legs open, filling her.

She closed her eyes, holding him tight, enjoying the

rocking of their bodies. Stars seemed to glitter behind her eyes and she opened them to center herself. Sloan kissed her deeply, his mouth hungrily devouring hers, and there was no centering herself.

She let the magic completely possess her.

OKAY. HE'D LOST his mind.

There was no other way to explain what he'd done last night. Sloan had slept with Kendall wrapped around him, his face buried in her hair. When he'd climbed from the bed to head out into the cold for the chores, he'd had to shove away the desire to linger, make love to her again. Kendall murmured a sleepy protest when he left, but he didn't allow her siren song to entice him.

He met his brothers in the barn. "Where's the scout?"

"Gone." Galen glanced his way. "Is that lipstick on your mouth?"

Sloan scrubbed a hand across his face. "Hell, no."

"Didn't think so." Galen slung a saddle onto a dark chestnut Thoroughbred and grinned. "You wouldn't fall for your assignment."

He wouldn't. Sloan grabbed a pitchfork and began tossing hay into stalls. "Gone where?"

"Falcon and Tighe are dropping him off somewhere." Galen's face gave nothing away. "It'll be a while before he makes it back this way."

Sloan nodded. "Good." Wherever his brothers took the scout, they'd be careful about not leaving tracks. "Did we get any info about who hired him?"

"Not much. Just what we already knew, which is that there are three mercs out there in the canyons, confirming the chief's count."

Sloan didn't feel comforted that there were only

three. "Had he managed to communicate any of our information or positions?"

"No. He claimed he was supposed to check in last night."

"Do we believe him?"

Galen shrugged. "It's irrelevant. What he'll let them know—when he gets out of the endless canyon he's taken to—is that we know about them. It will move the game forward more quickly than they wished."

Sloan turned. "What was his name?"

"Storm Cash. We found ID on him and Ashlyn was pretty good at getting information from him."

Sloan grimaced. "Was he Kendall's attacker?"

"Yeah. He meant to take her hostage. Figured she knew something about the family he could use. She fought harder than he expected, so things got a bit out of hand. I don't think he really meant to hurt her, but she's tough."

Kendall *was* tough. Tough-minded, tough in spirit. He admired that.

"You like her."

Sloan didn't glance at Galen. "I like everyone. Haven't you heard? I'm a really friendly guy."

His brother laughed. "That's a new one." He went off whistling. Sloan ignored Galen's assertion—or he tried. The truth was that he'd known Kendall for all of three days and he'd been unable to resist her.

She was clouding the mission, his mind, his heart.

After he finished his chores, Sloan went to the house to check on Kendall. He felt fairly safe with her being in the house during the day, because Fiona and Burke were always around. There was safety in numbers. Wasn't that what the chief had said?

Sloan hoped the nagging sensation would cease once he laid eyes on her.

Kendall wasn't in her room. She wasn't in the kitchen, nor her bath. Ignoring a flash of anxiety, he checked in the library.

"She went out," Fiona said from behind him. "Not that we wanted her to. I told her that Burke would go get whatever she needed. She said she was going stir-crazy."

"The roads are closed." Sloan frowned. "Where could she go?"

"Oh." Fiona waved a hand. "She's on the ranch. She went to take some photos of the area where the new bunkhouse will be. Said this was the perfect weather and conditions to show her how the light falls at certain times. Kendall said it was important to see that." Fiona nodded. "Light is very important to a home."

Sloan swallowed hard. "How did she go?"

"In the military jeep, although she talked about riding. I told her perhaps her leg wasn't healed enough for fighting through the snow on a horse, as stalwart as most of ours are." Fiona placed a fresh blackberry cobbler on the table. "Don't worry. Kendall's one of the smartest people I've ever met. She won't do anything to endanger herself. Mind you, I told her she should be resting, but Kendall's never in her life been in a bed for more than two consecutive days. Still, the intruder's been caught, so there's no danger at the moment. Right?"

Sloan shrugged on his oilskin. He went out the door without another word.

In his opinion, Kendall had already endangered herself. Fear stewed inside him, warning him that trouble was closer than he wanted it to be.

SLOAN SAW KENDALL right where she'd told Fiona she'd be. Staying back, he watched her, keeping himself hidden. She wouldn't take kindly to interference.

To her credit, Kendall stayed in the jeep as she took photos. She had a zoom lens on her camera. Every once in a while she checked the sky, factoring the light into her calculations.

He could almost hear her mind whirring with plans for the new bunkhouse. Jonas wouldn't have hired her if she wasn't the best. She would completely understand and execute his vision for Rancho Diablo and his other ranch, Dark Diablo.

She fascinated Sloan.

After ten more minutes of photographing the cold, snow-covered landscape, Kendall started the jeep and drove away. Sloan took a deep breath and turned his horse to follow the jeep tracks packing the snow.

He was going to give her hell for not noticing the hoofprints already in the jeep tracks as she returned to the ranch.

But he underestimated her. All of a sudden, the vehicle halted, then drove in a wide circle. She pulled up beside his horse, glaring at him.

"I don't need a bodyguard."

"Maybe you don't."

"You're carrying this caution too far," Kendall said. "The man who attacked me was caught." When Sloan didn't reply, she said, "Look, soldier. I'd rather have you as a lover than a bodyguard."

He blinked, completely caught off guard. "I guess it can't be both."

She shook her head. Sloan's heart sank a little. Her long hair was in a ponytail, covered by a blue ski cap. She had on a blue parka that matched her eyes. She wore some kind of black pants that looked warm and protected her injury.

"It can't be both because I left the house for ten minutes and you followed me. I'm carrying—a small gun, but enough to slow someone down—and I drove a jeep with all-wheel traction. I have my cell phone. Fiona knew where I was, as did Ashlyn." Kendall's frown didn't mar her beauty, but he felt it in his bones. "I've taken all the precautions. And yet here you are."

"You're my assignment," Sloan said.

After a long moment she nodded. "I know."

She started the jeep and drove off.

Sloan followed, wishing an assignment was all Kendall was to him. It would be so much easier that way.

KENDALL WAS IN BED when he went up to her room a few hours later. She was moving around photos she'd laid out on a board, but didn't look up. "I don't need a bodyguard."

"I got that message."

Her eyes met his. "So you don't need to be in my room."

That stopped him cold. "You want Ashlyn or one of my brothers to—"

"No. I don't." She put the photos on the nightstand, laid the board against the wall by the bed. "I'm not going to live in fear. I was scared because of what happened to me. I'm not going to be anymore."

"Okay." He didn't like it, but her decision had to be her own. He'd known making love to her was a mistake. It made casual, professional interaction between them impossible. "I'm going."

She nodded. "Thanks for understanding."

"I do." He looked at Kendall for a long moment,

wishing that he'd met her under different circumstances. "See you around."

He went out of her room, heading down the stairwell.

"Hi," Ashlyn said. "Where's Kendall?"

"Taking a nap." He didn't want to admit she'd given him his pink slip. "Where is everybody?"

Ashlyn smiled, went into the kitchen. She picked up a huge bowl of popcorn sitting on the counter. "Everybody's at their posts. Why aren't you at yours?"

She offered him the popcorn. He shook his head.

"I'm going to need a new post."

"You can take mine. I'm getting fat. If Fiona has a spare minute, she sticks something in the oven." His sister's eyes sparkled. "I weighed myself. I've actually gained three pounds. That's about a pound a day since we've been here."

"You could use it." He glanced at the ceiling, wondering what Kendall was doing. The problem with her running him off was that he wouldn't know what she was doing all the time. She was right in that respect: he'd been relying on his job as bodyguard for an excuse to be around her, see her. "Why'd you let her go out by herself?"

Ashlyn stared at him. "This isn't a prison, brother."

"Okay." He let out a breath. Maybe he was being paranoid. "Aren't we here to keep an eye on things?"

Ash munched some popcorn. "The family is gone. We're here in an overseer capacity now, more than anything."

She was right. He couldn't put Kendall in a bottle to keep her safe.

Xav came in, shaking snow from his shoulders as

he entered. "If this is any indication of what Christmas will be like, I predict it'll be white."

Sloan noticed his sister sat up straighter when Xav appeared. She offered him the popcorn bowl and Xav took a handful. The whole thing happened silently, as if this was a normal routine. Expected.

Sloan frowned, realizing his little sister might have a thing for Kendall's twin.

"Is this dinner?" Xav asked, his gaze on Ash.

"Maybe," she said, her eyes sparkling.

Sloan's radar went up. This wasn't like his sister. He couldn't remember her ever sparkling for a male before.

"How's my sister?" Xav asked Sloan.

"Independent."

He laughed. "I know. I'll go talk to her." He left the kitchen. Ash's gaze followed him, then returned to Sloan.

"Not a good idea," he said.

"Because it's not like you have eyes for Kendall or anything," Ash said sweetly.

Sloan drummed his fingers on the table for a second. Ash offered him the popcorn again. This time he shook his head. "It won't amount to anything."

Her brows rose. "That's your decision. No one says you have to be a eunuch."

He winced. That was one thing he wasn't. In fact, if he could head up the stairs and jump in bed with Kendall right now, he'd do it in a heartbeat.

"I think you're afraid of her," Ash said, wandering off with the popcorn. "She's really pretty nice, brother."

He shook his head. He knew just how nice she was. That was the problem.

"HOW'S THE LEG?"

Kendall smiled at her brother as he settled into the chair next to the window. "So much better. I have a bone to pick with you, by the way."

"Pick away." Xav propped his fingers in a steeple, grinning at her. "Does this have anything to do with the annoyed soldier downstairs? I swear I haven't made any big-brother noises about the two of you at all."

Kendall wagged a finger at him. "No changing the subject. And there's nothing to make noises about."

"Which is why he sleeps in your room at night." Xav nodded. "Makes perfect sense. He's just a great guy, and you're a nun."

Kendall ignored her brother's teasing. "I want to know what you thought you were doing early this morning. I saw you and some of the other Callahans drag that man into the bunkhouse. Tell me exactly what happened. You nearly gave me heart failure!"

Her brother looked pleased with himself. "There's nothing to tell. But you've got to know that it's a brother's privilege to have a small chat with a thug who sent his sister to the hospital."

"You've changed so much." Kendall shook her head. "I thought it was only Gage and Shaman who got sucked into Rancho Diablo. But you're all the way in now."

"You're not exactly staying away." Xav smiled at her. "I noticed you didn't ride out with the caravan to go back to the family compound."

She looked at her twin. "My job is here."

He clearly didn't believe her. "We run a global company. Your phone never stops ringing, even when you're lying in bed. Tell me why you can't do this job from Hell's Colony."

"I actually thought about leaving," Kendall admitted. "It would simplify things."

"And yet?"

She didn't want to. Not yet. "You win," she said softly. "I may have a slight crush on an outlaw."

Chapter Nine

When Sloan didn't come to her bed that night, Kendall told herself this was what she'd wanted. Space. Not to be just an assignment to him.

But the pull was too strong. Xav had recognized that her heart was becoming involved. Being housebound didn't help. Too much closeness made her think constantly about Sloan, which was dumb, because their lives were too different.

She packed her bag and texted Sloan.

I'm going to Hell's Colony to join the Callahan squad. Make sure the ranch stays in one piece now that it's been overrun by your family.

It seemed as if she waited a long time for his reply. Then she heard his boots on the stairs. He appeared in the doorway, tall and lean and devilish, and her heart jumped.

"It's probably for the best."

"Yes." She swallowed. "I just wanted to make sure you knew where I was going."

A small smile briefly crossed his lips before his

expression turned serious. Sloan reached out to run a strand of her hair through his fingers. "It's fine."

Then why did it not feel that way? Kendall pulled back from him and he let go of her hair. "I need to leave. Xav's going to take me to the airport."

Sloan picked up her hand and kissed it, old-world-style. Her heart beat harder at his touch. "I'll sleep better knowing you're safe."

She drew away, needing distance, and picked up her bag. "'Bye, soldier."

Sloan watched her walk out of the room. He was going to miss the heck out of her, yet he knew she'd be better off far away from here. He went down the stairs, not surprised to see his brothers grouped there and Ash hugging Kendall goodbye.

"It'll be just me and Aunt Fiona holding down the fort now," Ash said. "We don't even have enough girls for a good game of Old Maid."

Kendall laughed. "Our paths will cross again one day."

She hugged his brothers goodbye, then Xav helped her out to a truck with chain-wrapped tires. Sloan watched him gently make her comfortable in the back, propping up her leg on the bench seat.

Xav turned. "Want to ride with us, Ashlyn? Kendall probably wouldn't mind some female conversation. And I could use a shotgun rider on the way back."

Sloan stared as his sister eagerly jumped into the front seat.

They waved goodbye as Xav drove away. Sloan thought Kendall looked happy to be leaving.

Only after the taillights had dimmed in the distance did he go back inside.

"We might as well call a meeting," Falcon said. "Now that we caught one of them, we need a plan."

Sloan looked at his brothers. "Okay." It didn't seem right to meet in the upstairs library—the siblings still didn't feel like full-fledged Callahans—yet it made sense to stay in the house with Fiona and Burke. Fiona was, as usual, in the kitchen, stirring up something, and Burke was rolling out pie dough for her. "Let's go."

They trooped up to the library, easing into the leather chairs and sofa. He couldn't stop thinking about Kendall, and how much he wished she hadn't left.

If he hadn't made love to her, maybe she would have stayed.

He looked around the room. "Where do we start?"

Jace said, "We know the scout was only a preliminary attraction."

Falcon nodded. "He wasn't very effective. Look at his bumbling attempt on Kendall. With the element of surprise on his side, he should have been able to lock her down."

Sloan's blood ran cold. It didn't matter that his brother was telling him something he already knew—hearing it cut him deeply.

Galen went to the whiskey decanter, poured some into several tumblers. "And he cracked easily when we talked to him. Too easily."

"We think he was expendable," Tighe said, taking a glass from Galen. "They want us to know they're here."

"It's good that Kendall left," Dante said. "She was an easy target. And a distraction."

Didn't he know it. Sloan drank the whiskey, grateful for the liquid fire burning through him. "Now we just have Fiona and Burke."

Galen looked out the upstairs window, staring into

the darkness. "The snow has to be keeping our friends on ice out there."

Tighe walked to stand beside him. "They'll be hungry. And cold. Focused."

"If the weather stays this way for long, they may become restless. Prone to mistakes," Falcon said.

Sloan eyed his brothers. "We don't know how they trained. We don't know that they make mistakes. I wouldn't count on it. Jonas said the first merc they caught—Sonny—had lived in the canyons for years."

Dante nodded. "Let's keep our same posts, taking turns on the perimeter in teams. We'll leave Ash in the house with Fiona and Burke."

Jace set down his whiskey. "Or we flush them out. End this game. Go home."

Sloan blinked. "Home? This is home. According to the chief, we could be here for a long time."

Jace stood up and started pacing. "And then what? We endanger ourselves, fix the Callahans' problems and then ride away into the sunset?"

"They're family," Galen said. "They need us."

"I know," Jace said on a sigh. "Ignore me. I'm feeling caged."

"Remember what the chief told us," Falcon said. "One of us is the hunted one, if the chief is right. The only way to keep it together is to stick together."

"I'm sticking," Jace said. "But I've got questions, too. It's my nature."

Maybe they were *all* questioning something. Certainly Sloan didn't have any answers. He leaned against the bar, letting his gaze wander around the room. He could understand Jace's feelings. *Hell, I'm used to living in a cabin. Now I'm living in a palace and have made love to a princess. How's that for crazy?*

"Flushing them out would be the same as engagement," Sloan said. "Declaring open war."

"True," Falcon said. "That idea deserves consideration."

But they knew nothing about the enemy. "We need a scout of our own," said Sloan.

"They're going to be too smart to fall for something obvious." They'd be well trained; contract mercenaries weren't randomly chosen like fruit in a grocery store. Likely ex-military. He thought about the knife wound Kendall had suffered. Definitely a military-grade weapon. "I'll go."

His brothers stared at him.

"Why you?" Galen demanded.

"Because you're all soft," Sloan said.

He wasn't about to risk any of his own family, not after they were finally back together. It had been too many years. What the chief had done was bring them under one roof. Maybe they weren't a family like their cousins were, living tightly in a compound, where every day you saw the ones you loved. Maybe he hungered for that more than his brothers did.

Which would explain why Kendall had knocked him for a loop. And she had.

"Soft like doughnuts."

Jace laughed. "Excuse me, but one of us in this room has been sleeping in a nice comfy bed with a beautiful blonde. The rest of us have bunked where the beds don't have feather pillows." He grinned at him.

"I believe I saw Sloan once with sheet marks pressed into his delicate skin after he'd napped in the ivory tower," Falcon said.

Sloan held a hand up in surrender. "Okay, okay. I

had it pretty good for a night or two. I'll volunteer for the hard duty now."

Galen stood. "As the oldest, I should go."

"Nah," Sloan said, tensing, thinking about Galen out in the darkness with mercenaries. "We need a doctor on the ranch. A *live* doctor."

Falcon stood. "I'll go. I'm not as pretty as Kendall, but I can probably draw out some bored, cold, hungry—"

"You're pretty like the underside of my foot." Dante laughed. "I'm the only one who has any experience surviving without chocolate bonbons and lacy washcloths."

Tighe gave him a shove. "Sloan says he's going to be the fall guy. Don't make him feel self-conscious about his inexperience with survival conditions."

"Yeah. I'll pack my lacy washcloth and all will be cool." Sloan raised his head. "Let's figure out the battle plan, in case they bite."

Any further conversation was cut off by the sound of a window shattering right by his head. Sloan ducked, as did his brothers, hitting the ground, taking cover behind tables, drawing their guns.

"Rock," Galen said.

It was white and the size of a baseball. "Turn out the lights," Sloan said, and crouched to move to the wall.

He waited for a moment until his eyes adjusted to the darkness, then inched toward a window to peer out. A spotlight shone brightly on the thick snow. On a spotted Appaloosa, making no attempt to conceal himself, sat a man wearing a black felt Stetson and a long black coat. He waved, grinning, knowing someone was looking out at him and not caring that he was seen.

"Damn," Sloan murmured. "I'm going out there."

"I'll go, too," Galen said.

"Hell, all for one and one for all," Falcon said, following Sloan down the stairs.

"Tighe and Dante, you take sniper post," Sloan called back.

"On it," Dante called after him.

"Jace, you're backup," Sloan commanded, opening the front door.

"Right there," Jace said, moving to the den window off the kitchen.

Sloan, Galen and Falcon faced their visitor.

"Howdy, friends," the stranger said.

Sloan stiffened. "Friends usually bring a pie, not a rock."

The man laughed. "I don't bake much. And I don't know anything about a rock."

"The rock that just came through our window up there," Sloan said, playing along.

"Don't know a thing about that," the black-clad man said, his tone easy. "Just came by to welcome you to Rancho Diablo."

"Welcome us?" Sloan tensed. No one should have known they were there.

"Name's Storm Cash." He shifted on the big Appaloosa. "I own the ranch up the road."

Sloan felt his brothers tense in turn, coiled to spring.

"That's strange," Sloan said, his tone low and direct. "I met a man named Storm Cash yesterday."

"Did you?" The rider shrugged. "I'm the only one I know."

It was too coincidental. There was no way the scout they'd caught and this man had the same name. Someone was lying.

Sloan would bet this man was. He had a dark aura,

set off by the silvery spotlights. The sinister-looking scar across Storm's cheek might not represent anything more than a childhood accident. Long, jagged hair might not be a tell. A merc who didn't have a chance to visit a barber with any regularity would probably shave his head close, with a knife if necessary. Then again, the jagged ends might mean infrequent cuttings with a knife.

Sloan couldn't read him.

"Where'd you say you live, Cash?"

"Up the road." Storm jerked his head in the opposite direction of their other neighbor, Bode Jenkins.

"No one's mentioned we had new neighbors."

"Bought the place about six months ago. Someone told me to be sure and swing by to introduce myself to the Callahans."

Sloan kept silent. The story felt thin, but he didn't have anything concrete to go on.

"Too bad about your window. You want to fix that. Hear another snowstorm's on the way." He tipped his Stetson. "Nice to finally meet the Callahans."

"Yeah, about that. If you've been in Diablo for six months, why are you just stopping by now?" Sloan demanded.

"You know how a ranch takes your time from morning to night. But I'm sure we'll run across each other again soon." He turned the Appaloosa, patiently encouraging the animal to step over the snowdrifts to the main road.

"What do you think?" Falcon asked.

"Too easy." Their brothers joined them. The five stood watching silently as the man disappeared.

"I mean, why pay a visit at this hour?" Jace asked.

"Maybe he was on his way home from somewhere," Galen offered.

"Could be a neighborly sort. Our cousins are very social," Tighe said. "He may have heard that and thought nothing of checking in, with the weather as bad as it's been. It's a friendly thing to do among ranchers."

Sloan didn't like it. "We'd better go fix that window. Someone check on the old folks, too. And one of you go look in on the horses." He felt a huge responsibility to keep their cousins' home safe from harm. "If there's another storm coming in, the airport might close down."

"I've been checking Kendall's flight," Dante said, holding up his phone with a sheepish grin. "It left on time."

Sloan grunted, not surprised that Dante's quixotic mind had wondered about the weather and the flights. He wished he'd thought of it himself. Instead, all he thought about was Kendall's soft skin and how much he was going to miss her.

He looked at the sky, checking the movement of the clouds, and then followed his brothers inside. He didn't know what to make of their supposed neighbor, but he did know it was a good thing Kendall had gone home.

He had to think of nothing but the mission—not silky hair and the softest lips he'd ever kissed.

TWO MONTHS LATER, Christmas had come and gone. Christmas with the Callahans was always amazing, even if this year they weren't in their home. The group that had stayed at Dark Diablo had come to Hell's Colony so they could all be together. Kendall was pretty certain this was the best Christmas she'd ever experienced. Shaman and Gage had come home, too, with their families, which had thrilled their mother. Everyone but Xav had made it back.

"All my life I thought our house was too enormous and, in some ways, not really lived in," Kendall told Jonas. "With your family here, it feels like a real home."

"Wasn't it always?" Jonas asked.

"Well, we run our business from here, so we have rooms and a guesthouse for any clients or lawyers that might need to stay over." Kendall smiled. "It's the first time we've used almost every single bedroom."

Jonas raised a brow. "This is why you're perfect to oversee the building of the new bunkhouse. You understand large scale."

"The architect sent the plans over. I'll get your opinion on them soon. I think you'll be pleased. And building is slated to begin in March."

Jonas smiled. "You deserve a raise. You should ask your boss for one."

"I will." Kendall went off to check on the kids, most of whom were playing in what had been the formal parlor, an all-white room with only an ebony piano to relieve the icy formality. For the season, Kendall had had a twelve-foot-tall Christmas tree brought in, draping it with colored lights and red bows and candy canes—and a huge sparkling star on the top.

The children had loved it.

This room would never again be a fancy parlor. Kendall grinned, watching the kids run their toy trucks and remote cars over the white marble floor. She'd never realized how much fun children could be. It was a strange thing for her to think, because she'd always been dead set against having children herself.

But it might not be so bad to be a mother. She

looked at all the Callahan wives, seeing how happy they were—and then it hit her like a winter blizzard.

She hadn't had a period this month.

Chapter Ten

Just when he thought his feelings for Kendall had been an amazing fantasy of a man who had been too long without a woman, Sloan learned just how deep inside him Kendall had gotten.

"Hi," she said, sitting at the kitchen table as if she'd never been away.

Fiona grinned and put a tray of gingerbread cookies on the counter near Sloan. She took off her apron, her eyes merry with laughter. "I'm going to go kiss Handsome," she said, and went off to hunt for Burke.

"What are you doing here?" Sloan asked, ignoring the startled leap of his heart at seeing Kendall. God, he'd missed her.

"I have a job, remember? Building on the bunkhouse starts next month."

True. By the way his heart was banging around in his chest, clearly he'd hoped she'd come back because of him. "It's good to see you."

She picked up a cookie, gave him a sideways look, but didn't say anything.

The ball was in his court. "It really is good to see you."

She laid the cookie on a napkin in front of her. "We

don't have to be friendly with each other, Sloan, beyond the ordinary hello, goodbye."

He supposed he deserved that. He'd run her off, hadn't he? And it didn't matter that he'd been right—she had been safer elsewhere. But it was obvious she didn't hold him in high esteem for his caution.

It was even more obvious that the sexual side of their friendship was never happening again.

"I'm pregnant," Kendall said, and Sloan felt as if the floor dropped out from beneath him.

"What?"

"Pregnant." She hesitated. "I didn't mean to blurt it out. I wanted to tell you in person. I thought of a million ways I could say it." She looked at him, and Sloan was conscious only of the craziest feelings running through him: shock, fear, joy, insane lust. "I didn't mean to tell you so ungracefully."

He blinked, frozen.

"I know you're stunned," Kendall said softly. "Believe me, I was, too. I still am."

He leaned against the wall, staring at the most beautiful woman he'd ever seen, who was telling him she was pregnant. His mind was completely blown. It was like nothing he'd ever experienced.

"I know it was just one night," Kendall added. "Clearly, my diaphragm didn't hold up to the task."

"I'm going out now," Sloan finally said, after a long moment during which she was afraid he might not say anything at all. "And then we're going to talk, you and I."

Her eyes widened. She had no idea how badly he wanted to kiss her. Take her upstairs and make love to her again and again.

He had to control the emotions swamping him. She

didn't feel the same way about him that he felt about her. It was obvious by her coolness. She might not even want him involved with the baby. Which would kill him.

He had to be very careful. She was tough, she was brave and independent, and she didn't need him.

He needed *her.*

Sloan jammed his hat on his head and went out into the cold January night.

Fiona came back into the kitchen five minutes after Sloan left, which was good, because Kendall definitely didn't want to be alone with her thoughts.

"Did you tell him?" she asked.

"I did. Not very gently, I'm afraid." Kendall smiled. "I handled it more like a business conversation than a bombshell."

"Hmm." Fiona pondered that for a moment. "Let's have some tea."

She picked up a blue-willow-patterned teapot, filling it with water from the copper kettle that was almost always sitting on low heat for whoever might come in and want a cup of tea, then placed sugar and milk on a wooden tray decorated with a beautiful Santa Fe-style runner. Kendall joined her at the long family dinner table, glad for the female companionship.

"What did Sloan say?" Fiona asked, as they took teacups from the tray and filled them with the steaming brew.

"Not much. He said we'd talk later. Then he left." Kendall smiled a bit sadly. "He looked like I probably did when I saw that blue line on the pregnancy test."

Fiona smiled, sipped her tea. "Well, things have a

way of working out. And he's had a lot on his mind, keeping things together around here."

The door blew back open, startling both of them. Sloan came inside, not even stopping to stomp the snow off his boots—which he always did—or dust off his coat. He walked to the table, his gaze on Kendall.

"Marry me," he said.

Kendall didn't move, but as she stared into his dark blue Callahan eyes, she was conscious of a shocking desire to say yes. *Gladly, yes.*

Which wasn't like her at all. She wasn't the kind of woman to do anything impetuous.

"I think I'll carry some tea up to Burke," Fiona said. "Maybe some gingerbread cookies. He has such a sweet tooth at this time of the evening."

She left, humming under her breath. Kendall barely realized Fiona hadn't taken any tea or cookies with her. "Sloan. You're...not thinking straight."

"I *know*. It's impossible to think straight." He paced a few steps before turning around to look at her. "I'm going to be a father. Am I supposed to be able to think straight?"

Kendall looked down at her hands. "It took me a few weeks to wrap my head around the idea that I'm going to be a mother."

"You've known for a while?" Sloan demanded. "Why haven't you told me before?"

"It's not the kind of thing one drops on someone over the phone," Kendall said. "It was the holidays, for one thing, and I know you've been busy—"

"Don't do that again," Sloan said. "Please. If you have something to say, just tell me. I like your direct approach. I'm not the kind of guy who needs information fed to him. Just the facts, ma'am." He sank into the chair across from her. "Marry me, Kendall."

"Why?" People got married when they were in love. She and Sloan were not in love. Lust was very different from love.

"Because we're having a baby," Sloan said. "That's why we're going to get married."

"I'm too old to do things for the sake of reputation."

"I've never done anything for the sake of reputation," Sloan said. "I never had a reputation except in the military. I'm not thinking of reputations. I'm thinking about our child, who's going to want to know who his father is. That his father's going to be around. I'll teach him to ride, and how to shoot a bow and arrow, and how to find the proper medicinal herbs in the wild…. What?"

Kendall shook her head. "You can do all that without us being married, Sloan. And it goes without saying that our baby will probably be a girl, which you'll richly deserve. Soften up that alpha-male gene, fractionally."

He ignored all that. "If you don't want to stay married to me after the baby's born, that will be your choice. But it's not a choice for the baby not to have the Callahan name."

Kendall blinked. She hadn't thought of it in those terms.

"I'll have to locate a *hitaathli*. I'll have to ask the chief if there's one around here."

She didn't even know where he was from, not to mention what a *hitaathli* was. Kendall assumed it was some kind of Navajo ceremonial overseer, and tried to envision herself wearing an Oscar de la Renta bridal gown to a Navajo wedding. She'd never really thought about getting married, so it wasn't as if she had preconceived notions of what she wanted. Still, the differences between Sloan and her were many.

There was absolutely no reason the two of them should get married.

Except that in her heart, Kendall knew he was a good man, a man of honor, and he intended to do right by her child. She had plenty of money, didn't need financial help.

She didn't need anything.

But she *wanted* Sloan.

It wasn't enough to base a marriage on.

All her life she'd been Gil Phillips's daughter, struck from the same mold as her tough-minded corporate father. And now she was being offered the chance to be swept off her feet, throw all caution and prevailing logic to the wind, and find out what was on the other side of *yes* with this hunky, mysterious man.

She put her hand over Sloan's. "I'm not an easy person to live with."

He looked at her. "You're not an easy person to live without. Anyway, you'll get better with time."

"*I'll* get better with time?"

"Sure. Motherhood is known to improve most women."

"You're not much of a chauvinist, are you?"

He laughed. "There's not one bit of chauvinist in my entire body. I just want to take care of you and my child. That's not chauvinism."

Kendall lowered her gaze, thinking that Sloan was actually very sexy in his rather autocratic way.

"I *am* slightly pigheaded," Sloan said. "My brothers are pretty generous with their synonyms for that term, so I know it's probably true. The good thing is that fatherhood is known to change a lot of men for the better, too, so it wouldn't be completely unlikely that fatherhood might have a beneficial effect on me. It's a risk, but it could happen. You'll just have to take a leap of faith and find out."

By the sparkle in his eyes, Kendall figured Sloan knew very well that he was a bit more than simply pigheaded. "You'll be leaping, too."

"I know. And my leap has a helluva longer drop than yours, lady." He turned his hand up into hers, then lifted her fingers to his lips, brushing them briefly. "So we're agreed? I'll talk to Grandfather about finding a *hitaathli*. We'll marry as soon as I can locate one."

He assumed she'd say yes. Kendall looked at Sloan for a long time, gazing into his eyes, then got up.

She was never going to get over the feelings she had for him. Time apart had done nothing to alleviate her desire, the emotions she felt when he touched her.

"Yes," she said.

He nodded.

There was nothing else to say. Kendall went upstairs to her room and looked out the window, seeing Xav and Ashlyn walking a black horse between them. Working together, as a team.

She and Sloan were going to make a very strange team.

"YOU'RE GETTING MARRIED?" Dante stared at him, as did his other brothers as they loafed in the upstairs library. Ash never loafed. She was more deceptively elegant, belying her strength and quickness.

The shattered window had been repaired long ago, the shards cleared away. Sloan still had his doubts about their strangely friendly neighbor, but for the moment, he had other things on his mind.

"Did hell freeze over?" Galen asked.

"It is colder than a bear's hiney outside," Tighe observed, "and the temperatures will drop more. Maybe hell did freeze over."

"Who's the lucky girl?" Jace asked.

Sloan sighed, sipped his whiskey for courage. "Kendall Phillips."

His brothers laughed. Then sobered as they saw the serious look on Sloan's face.

"You can't settle down," Ash said. "Of all my brothers, you're the least suitable for a woman like that. Too many rough edges." She grinned at him mischievously.

"It's probably true," Falcon said. "Does Kendall know you're a loner? Not suited to matrimony or anything else that requires sociability?"

"Ha, ha, ha," Sloan said, not surprised by the generous ribbing he was receiving. "I think she's seen my best points."

His family gazed at him silently.

"Well, congratulations," Galen said, getting up to shake his hand and pound his back. The other brothers followed, and Sloan felt mildly better, even if he'd left out one small detail.

"I'm not congratulating you," Ash said. "I can tell you're not telling us the whole truth. It's in your eyes, dear brother. I can read them like a book."

"Maybe he's turned into a romantic overnight," Galen said. "It could happen."

"And pigs could fly if they had wings." Ash leaned forward, staring at him, her short, spiky hair giving her an elfin appearance. "Tell little sister the truth."

Sloan swallowed. "Just seems like the right time to settle down."

She made a sound of disgust. "I have my suspicions."

He nodded. "That's fine."

"The thing is, all my brothers are very readable." Ash seemed to be talking to herself. "Falcon, he's brilliant, right? A poet and out-of-the-box thinker. At thirty-three, you can think a lot of cool stuff, maybe even about settling down, so I could see him convincing himself somehow that marriage is a good thing."

"Not me," Falcon said defensively. "Don't put that on me."

"And Galen, he's the oldest. He's driven, and as an allopathic doctor and medicine man, he might want to find a lady." Ash nodded, ignoring Falcon. "Or Jace. Jace is thirty, but he's been talking for a while about settling down. He wants to find someone to share his hopes and dreams. If he wasn't such a knucklehead, he just might do it."

Ash ticked them off on her fingers. "Okay, Tighe, we can forget about. He'll never let a woman tie him down. You're too crazy." She smiled at Tighe fondly. "But your twin, Dante, he's a thinker and a trickster. He's the one I can count on to do something crazy, like go off on a bender to Australia and marry some gorgeous Aussie native. Maybe even Africa. Something really unexpected and faraway and crazy-romantic. But you, Sloan, dearest brother, you're not cut out for the married life. You're a loner, and you resent the hell out of authority. How are you ever going to share anything with a woman? Especially a woman like Kendall, who's very outgoing and social?"

All of his brothers had been enjoying Ash's roasting until their own names got called; now they wore slightly perplexed, maybe even annoyed, expressions. Sloan laughed. "It's easy. She caught me fair and square."

"How?" Tighe asked. "I want to know how so I can avoid a woman with catching on her mind."

"Yeah," Falcon said. "Because we didn't see a whole lot of romancing going on around here. If it's one of those sneaks-up-on-you things, I really want to be on my guard."

Sloan sighed, then stood. "I'm going to bed. Early to bed, early to rise, makes a man healthy, wealthy and wise."

"Or it makes him a *father*," Ash said. "You're going to be a dad!"

He hadn't figured he could keep anything from Ash. She leaped into his arms, not even waiting for him to confirm her suspicions before raining kisses and hugs on him. "My big brother's going to have a baby!"

The others sat very still. Ash undraped herself from around his neck. "You're going to be *uncles*. Don't you have anything to say to Sloan? Or are you just going to sit there and ignore the fact that the Chacon Callahans are starting a new branch of the family tree?"

His brothers appeared blindsided, shell-shocked, dazed.

"Is she right?" Jace asked.

Sloan nodded. "It's true."

"Whoa," Dante said. "We just sent all the kids off, to keep them safe. Now you'll be the one with the precarious situation, bro. It's easier to grab a newborn than just about anything, probably. But congratulations, man. Not sure how you did it—or when—but that's awesome." Dante slapped him on the back, and everyone else followed suit. But the celebration was just a bit muted.

It was true. Sloan was a loner. He was marrying a woman who'd never been alone, having been surrounded by a loving family and a company that took her around the world. He did resent authority, and Kendall had been right—he was overprotective, overbearing and kind of, well, possessive.

Which wasn't going to get tamed any if he had a baby to worry about. Sloan's teeth ground together as he thought about how much everything had changed. Before, he'd only had Kendall to worry about losing. Now, he was going to have something else very important and precious to fear losing, as well. Two parts of his life.

"I'm going out for a while," he said, hurrying from the library as fast as he could. He had to be alone, needed to think—

No. Ingrained habits were bad. He had to change some of his. He needed to be with Kendall—not be alone with his fears and doubts.

He walked down the hall toward Kendall's room before he could change his mind.

Chapter Eleven

Kendall looked up at Sloan looming in her doorway. "Change your mind, soldier?"

"No." He sat in the chair he'd used when her leg was injured. "Maybe we should iron out some details."

She closed her laptop. "Go for it."

"I'm possessive."

"Really. I didn't know that."

"Not in a weirdo, freaky way or anything," he said hurriedly. "More protective, I guess."

"And I'm really independent." Kendall waited for him to digest that.

"Yeah." He scratched his head, then shoved his hand back through his dark hair. "There have been developments since you left. So it's not like I want to bother your independence, but now there'll be two of you here."

She nodded. "I know. I don't have to stay after we get…married." It was hard to say that. She didn't know how to tell her mother, her brothers. Imagining herself as a wife seemed so foreign. "Actually, I have an ultrasound scheduled in a few weeks, so I'd be leaving, anyway."

"Okay. I just want you to know I'm going to try hard

to be…calm. Rational." Sloan shifted, and Kendall felt surprised by how much it meant to her that he cared enough to battle his own personal demons.

"Thank you. I really can take care of myself."

"I know." He backed out of the room, his boots thumping on the rug-covered stairs.

She pulled open the window, staring down in case he went outside. When he appeared below, heading at a good clip for the bunkhouse, she said, "Sloan!"

He glanced up. "Yeah?"

"We don't have to do this, you know."

He shrugged. Then he grinned. "Maybe it won't be as horrible as I think it will be."

She couldn't shrug off with a smile something as important as marriage. "Maybe it will, though. Or worse."

"You're going to have to decide if you can deal with your own fears. I can handle an opinionated woman. Have you met my sister?"

Kendall supposed she deserved that, after giving him grief about all his faults. "No one's ever called me opinionated," she said, fibbing just a bit.

"I doubt that, Barbie," he said, laughing as he walked away.

The next time she was outside, he was going to get smacked with the snowball of all snowballs.

Especially since he hadn't even gotten close to kissing her—and she really wished he would.

AFTER HOURS OF NOT BEING able to sleep, Kendall texted Sloan. Are you awake?

She got an immediate reply. Yes. Is something wrong?

Her phone glowed in the darkness, the words mocking her. *You promised you wouldn't be a worrywart.*

Instantly, her phone rang. She hit the answer key. "Can't a girl just want to talk?"

"I don't know," Sloan said. "You're pregnant. We're in a house where…"

He stopped. She frowned, wondering what he was keeping from her. "Never mind. I'm not in the mood to talk anymore."

"I'm new to this," Sloan said. "You're going to have to let me ease into this new me slowly."

"The relaxed you who doesn't panic every time I text you in the middle of the night?" She heard him on the stairs. "I'm going to remember that you're like a genie in a bottle. Except always in full panic mode."

He came into the room. "I'm not panicked. But we've had our unique surprises here at Rancho Diablo. I'd rather be safe than sorry."

He pulled off his boots, and she felt his weight sink into the bed. Kendall put her phone on the nightstand. "What are you doing?"

"You wanted to talk. So we'll talk. Only you're going to do it very quietly, because I have to be up in about four hours."

He eased into the bed, bringing a bit of outdoor chilliness into the warm sheets with him. Kendall froze, waiting to see what he would do next. But he flopped over on his side, just as he had the first night, his back to her. "I'm listening."

Now that he was here, she realized she wanted more than a listening ear. This man was going to be her husband—and yet their relationship was anything but close. "I was wondering what to wear when we get married."

"You're lying awake thinking about clothes?" Sloan chuckled. "I don't care what you wear."

Silence met his words. Sloan waited for her to continue the conversation, get to the point of what was really on her mind, but when Kendall didn't speak again, he realized his comment had probably not been taken in the spirit in which he meant it.

Rolling over, he wrapped an arm around her waist. "It's a fairly simple ceremony. There'll be some words spoken, maybe some blue cornmeal eaten, depending on who does the ceremony. But there's no prescribed dress code. It's different from other cultures, not as elaborate. So you wear whatever makes you happy. You'll be beautiful no matter what you wear, babe."

Silence met his words again, and Sloan wondered if he'd erred again. But then she said, "That's so sweet, Sloan," and he grinned in the darkness.

"It's true. You're the most beautiful woman I've ever laid eyes on. It hasn't quite hit me that you're going to be my wife. My brothers and sister are giving me fits about it."

"Why? Don't they think we should get married?"

He rolled her over so he could kiss her, letting his lips linger against hers. "They're jealous."

"They're not," she said, giggling.

"I'm pretty sure they are. But they lie like rugs. They'd never admit they wish they were getting married and having a family."

He kissed her again, his heart racing, his body responding, and she wrapped her arms around his neck, pulling him close. Sloan thought he might die of happiness, if she didn't kill him with worry first.

Two weeks later, Sloan and Kendall stood under a scraggly mesquite tree, the sun shining lightly on them, chasing the cold away. The canyons made a beautiful backdrop of dusky tans and deep reds, and Sloan couldn't believe he was marrying the amazing woman beside him. Kendall had resolved her worries about what to wear, settling on a soft, filmy gown of un-adorned white that fell straight to her ankles, clinging to her curves on the way down. It was simple and per-fect. She'd put her hair up with a turquoise barrette, and wore a fringed white shawl that draped down her back.

He couldn't stop smiling.

The *hitaathli* who performed the ceremony said a few words, then Sloan and Kendall fed each other some blue cornmeal. They hadn't invited anyone except her brothers and his family, and Fiona and Burke, yet the small gathering felt perfect to Sloan. He figured the simple ceremony was very different from what Ken-dall might have envisioned she might one day have. Even the rings were simple: silver bands, hers with tiny pieces of turquoise worked into a flower pattern.

He kissed her, so she'd know he understood if she had reservations. Kendall surprised him by putting her arms around his neck. She whispered, "It was a beau-tiful ceremony."

A smile lit his face. He couldn't help it. How did an outlaw like him end up with a woman who made him smile constantly?

SLOAN WAS STILL SMILING a week later when he took Ken-dall to her doctor's appointment. He was really looking forward to the ultrasound.

His bride was nervous. "I hope everything is all right."

"The baby is fine. Don't worry." He wasn't going to share that he felt so jittery he felt as if he was back in a war zone. He hadn't had nerves all the time then, but every now and again he'd experienced overwhelming emotions he'd had to work hard to gather in. That was how he felt right now: filled with so many feelings he had to breathe deep, control his thoughts, keep everything tight. "You're a wonderful mother."

She smiled. "I hope I will be."

He nodded. "You will."

The doctor came in, wearing a smile. "Ready to see your baby?" Dr. Adele asked.

Kendall could barely reply. She was so excited—so anxious, too—she could hardly wait. Sloan squeezed her fingers as they began the procedure.

"Now what you'll see first," Dr. Adele said, "if you look right here, are healthy twins. Obviously fraternal, because this is separate from this here. Can you see that?" she asked, glancing at them, her eyes shining.

"Did you say twins?" Kendall said.

"I did." Dr. Adele laughed. "Congratulations."

Kendall looked at Sloan—and burst into tears.

He gathered her to him, and Kendall sprouted water like a faucet. "I'm so sorry. I don't know why I'm crying."

Dr. Adele continued to look at the screen. "Hormones. And the surprise. You're newlyweds, right?"

Kendall nodded, pulled herself together and off of Sloan's chest, even if he felt so good she really didn't want to. He rubbed her back soothingly, and Kendall tried to conduct herself more calmly and less emotionally. "We got married last week."

"This is an adjustment." The doctor got up. "Twins are always a surprise, and require more planning than for one baby. I have twins," Dr. Adele said, smiling. "Identical twins. It's love times two. But it's important to keep the lines of communication open between you."

"We will," Kendall said, wondering how they'd do that when they were still figuring out how they related to each other.

The obstetrician smiled. "I'll see you in my office. There's some information you'll need for the next few months."

"Thank you," Kendall said, and the doctor left.

Sloan sat back. "I guess we shouldn't be surprised. You're a twin. Dante and Tighe are twins. We're lucky we're not having quadruplets, I suppose."

Kendall gasped. "Don't say it!"

He laughed. "This is going to be fun."

"Fun?" She crooked a brow. "For who?"

"Both of us," he said. "Maybe me more than you."

Kendall blew her nose. "I'd better approve those architect plans before I get too big to do anything."

He laughed. "Only my business-minded wife would worry more about her job than the fact that she's now going to need two of everything."

Kendall looked up. "I'm trying not to freak out." She really was. Where was she going to raise these children? It couldn't be at Rancho Diablo—not with things the way they were. She was going to have to go back to Hell's Colony.

Which didn't seem like the best thing for a blossoming marriage. As Dr. Adele said, communication was important. Sloan was trying to act as though he wasn't Mr. Panic Attack, but Kendall knew him too well. Yesterday she'd gone for a short, gentle horseback ride by herself and he'd sent Ashlyn to "keep her company." She wouldn't have been so suspicious of that except later, when she'd gone for a walk to the end of the road, he'd sent Tighe to "check the roads." Which just happened to be where she was walking.

"You're not fooling me," she said. "I know you're going to breathe into a paper bag as soon as I turn my back."

He grinned, a devil in blue jeans. "No. What I'm going to do is go into the doctor's office, let her tell us everything we need to know about having twins, and then I'm going to ask her if I can still make love to my wife."

Kendall's breath caught. "I was going to ask her how long I could make love to my husband."

He kissed her hand. "Let's tell Dr. Adele to keep her speech short. We have things to do."

SLOAN HADN'T BEEN completely truthful with his wife. Things had been quiet around the ranch, but he and his brothers and Ash had agreed it felt like the calm before the storm. Not one, but two babies would make Kendall a considerable target.

He doubted she'd appreciate his worries, so he kept them to himself. The lovemaking was too sweet for him to do much complaining.

"Hey," Galen said, walking into the old bunkhouse. "You look grim."

"I'm having twins. Grim isn't how I feel. Turned inside out, maybe."

Galen laughed. "Congratulations. Better you than me."

"Your turn is coming one day." Sloan paced to a window, staring out at the icy landscape. "The snow's getting on my nerves."

"Spring's a while off." Galen kicked back onto the leather sofa, his expression serious. "I probably don't have to tell you that Kendall shouldn't be at Rancho Diablo."

"I know." Sloan was trying to figure out how to tell her. "Kendall isn't the kind of woman who takes those types of suggestions with enthusiasm."

Galen smiled. "I like you falling for a woman who isn't cowed by your gruff demeanor."

Sloan grunted. "Did I say I've fallen for her?"

"You just worry about her 24/7."

"It's a job."

"Mmm. Keep telling yourself that." Galen cracked open a beer. "Want one?"

Sloan shook his head. "I'm taking Kendall out to dinner tonight in Diablo. She said she's going to be on bed rest in a few months, so she doesn't want to be stuck inside the house all winter."

Galen walked to a window, staring out. "I don't blame her. Where is she right now?"

"Taking a nap. Said she wanted beauty sleep before we went out tonight."

Galen laughed. "That's what she told you."

Sloan looked up. "What do you mean?"

"Far be it from me to rat out my beautiful sister-in-law, but I think she just took off."

Sloan hopped to his feet, staring out the window. "I'll see you later."

Galen's laughter followed him outside.

SLOAN FOLLOWED the tire tracks of the military jeep at a slow pace, reminding himself that Kendall and he had had this battle before, and she hadn't appreciated his vigilance.

Maybe she was right. He did tend to overdo on caution. That caution had saved him many times. Special Ops was no place to be without a good dose of second sense.

He figured he knew where she was heading, and sure enough, she went right to the area where the new bunkhouse skeleton had been marked off with wood stakes and small flags. The ground was too frozen now to begin digging the basement Jonas was determined to have. Sloan thought he'd heard Kendall say that phase was slated for March.

It would probably kill her to be housebound during the building of her pet project.

He found a strip of uneven canyon ledge and waited, scanning the landscape for anything out of the ordinary. It felt quiet, too quiet. No hawks circled in the distance. The snow blanketing the canyons reflected the sunlight despite the occasional cloud.

Kendall got out of the jeep, walking the wood frame marking the site. Every once in a while she stood back to take a photo, jot down a note. He understood why Jonas had hired her to oversee the redo of Rancho Diablo and Dark Diablo, his property in Tempest, New Mexico. She was entirely dedicated to her work.

He heard hooves making their way through the ice-laced snow, and Storm Cash rode up from the west, stopping at Kendall's side. Sloan tensed, pulled his gun. Waited. Leveled the semi at Storm's wide back.

"What the hell are you doing?" Ash asked at his elbow, and Sloan bit back a curse.

"I could have shot him," he told his sister, not entirely surprised that she'd sneaked up on him. It was a specialty she was proud of—the ability to make absolutely not one whisper of sound. They'd had contests when they were kids, held by their parents and other elders. It had been a game—until their parents had gone away.

But Sloan knew the way he and his sibling had

grown up had toughened them. "I could have jumped and pulled the trigger."

"You're not twitchy," Ash whispered. "You're a lot of things, but twitchy isn't one of them. Besides, the lock is on."

He cursed again. Took the lock off and leveled the gun once more, his gaze on Storm and Kendall. "What are you doing here?" he asked, never moving his eyes.

"Finding out why you're off post. Falcon sent me looking for you. He said you hadn't called for backup. You're not supposed to be out here, and I'm pretty sure the family's going to gnaw on your ears about it when you get back."

"That's fine." Sloan didn't really care at the moment. All he could focus on was his wife, the woman carrying his twins, who had no business being out in the snow with a possible merc.

"Hey, check it out. Kendall's wearing real boots. With rubber soles and everything. Functional. I didn't know she did functional." Ash laughed. "Did you buy those for her?"

He hadn't. While it was surprising to see his wife in something other than sky-high, bright-colored pumps or stylish boots, he didn't care about that right now, either. Storm was having way too much fun talking to his wife, his hearty laughter floating over to them even at this distance. "What do you suppose he wants?"

"To make trouble." Ash moved around Sloan. "I'll see what he's up to. And keep you off Kendall's bad side. You know she doesn't like it when you crowd her space."

"I'm not— Whatever. Go."

His sister headed toward the pair still chatting away as if there wasn't anything to be concerned about.

Maybe there wasn't. Storm might be just an average neighbor out to be friendly. It wasn't entirely uncommon on big spreads, where visits between neighbors were infrequent enough to warrant a conversation. In a village, there was no such thing as stepping outside a hogan without seeing one's friends.

Sloan could see Storm's white teeth and huge smile when Ash walked up and stood next to Kendall, and it irritated the hell out of him, though he couldn't have said why. Everything about the man annoyed him, but when he started getting annoyed about a man's teeth, then Sloan was ticked on a deep level.

He was jealous. "That's just great," he muttered. "That'll win me points with my wife." She'd just love a jealous husband watching her every move. At least that's the way she'd see it.

He had to get better control of himself.

Kendall got back into the jeep and Ash joined her. Storm watched them drive away, his gaze on them for a long time. Kendall passed Sloan's location, and Ash didn't even glance his way—she was too well trained for giveaway tells.

Then he looked at Storm, and even though he knew it was impossible, Sloan had the strangest feeling that the man knew he was there, and had known all along.

Which was trouble.

Chapter Twelve

"You can't go off post without telling us," Falcon said when Sloan returned.

"I know. I wasn't expecting to." He knew he deserved the dressing-down from his brothers. They all sat in the bunkhouse, wearing stern, annoyed expressions.

"If Galen hadn't seen you leave, we'd have had a hole in coverage. The enemy is patient. They wait for those kinds of opportunities." Tighe's face was stoic, but his words held ominous warning that was right on target.

Sloan knew that, too. "I don't expect it to happen again." It wouldn't. He had to talk to Kendall, tell her that when she said she was going to take a nap to freshen up for their dinner date— "Hellfire! I've got to go." He shot off the sofa, not wanting to be late picking up his wife for their first date. He was pretty certain lateness wasn't something wives looked upon with favor.

He definitely wanted Kendall looking on him with favor.

"Wait." Jace stopped his headlong rush to the door. "Bro, we have to tell you something."

He glanced at his vintage military wristwatch. With

luck, Kendall was the type of woman who took a long time to get ready. "Can you make it quick?"

"Brother," Dante said, "she's got to go."

"Who's got to— Oh." He looked around at his brothers' faces.

"Kendall can't stay here." Tighe wore an expression of sympathy, but determination, too. "It's dangerous. And your attention is divided."

It was true. He hated to admit it. He'd won medals for his service, made the tribe and his family proud. "I think it's the twins," he said. "Being a dad has my mind twirling around like pinwheels in my head."

"Maybe," Galen said. "All the more reason Kendall should return home to her family, and the Callahans. Where she will be safe, and the children, too."

His family was right. They were a team, they knew each other as well as they knew the spirits of their ancestors. Sloan swallowed. Took a deep breath, sighed. "I'll tell her tonight."

Jace let him pass. Sloan headed across to the main house, his heart heavy.

Dreading what he had to do.

"So TELL ME ABOUT YOURSELF," Kendall said, laughing as she did so. They'd settled into a diner in town called Banger's Bait and Tackle, which served a mean catfish. She didn't know if Sloan liked catfish, but this was a quiet, family-style restaurant, which suited her, because she intended to spend time getting to know her very handsome, very sexy husband. "I guess that sounds strange, since we're married."

His navy eyes seemed worried. He didn't smile at her ridiculous-sounding question. "It takes time to get to know someone. A long time."

"I feel like I've known you forever, in some ways," Kendall said softly. "I don't know why, but something about you seems very comfortable to me." He shifted, his leather jacket stretching across his broad shoulders as he moved. "So we'll start small. Tell me about your parents. I guess I'll meet them one day."

Sloan shook his head. "No. We don't see them."

"Never?"

"No."

He didn't seem inclined to elaborate. Kendall frowned, thinking family information wasn't an unusual topic for married people to share.

"Did you not get along?"

"We got along. They were wonderful parents." He drummed his fingers on the table, glanced around the restaurant. The waitress came over, a bouncy redhead named Mabry, who took their drink orders.

"My dad's name is Carlos Chacon," he continued when she'd left. "My mother's name is Julia Connally. She was from Orange County, Virginia. They met on a military base in Germany. Love at first sight." Sloan drank his beer when it arrived, then set it down. Kendall sipped her Perrier, hoping he'd reveal more.

He frowned, and Kendall wondered why, then understood when Storm Cash walked over to their table.

"We meet again," he said to Kendall. He reached out to shake Sloan's hand. "Callahan."

Sloan didn't take his hand. "What do you want, Cash?"

Kendall's eyes widened. Her husband was being a bit rude to one of their neighbors, and it surprised her.

"Just being neighborly," Storm said.

"No need." Sloan glared at Storm, his expression fierce.

"Ever find out who broke your window?" Storm asked.

"Funny thing, but that rock didn't talk."

Sloan sipped his beer, seemingly casually, but Kendall knew better. He was tense, more so than usual.

Cash tipped his hat to her. "Evening, ma'am."

"Goodbye." Kendall watched as Storm walked away, and then turned her gaze to Sloan. "What was that all about?"

He shrugged, opened his menu.

"Sloan."

His gaze met hers. "Yes?"

She pointed toward Storm's retreating back. "Explain. The attitude, the broken window and rock part of the story."

"Someone threw a rock through the library window late one night. Cash happened to be in the neighborhood."

Storm had seemed so nice. Kendall studied her husband. "Do you know that he did it?"

"No. I'm going to have a steak. What appeals to you?"

"Sloan, this doesn't feel like a date when you're hiding behind your menu and avoiding telling me things. It's hard to feel like we're married when you don't mention rocks flying through windows." She wondered if he was annoyed with her for speaking to Storm. But how was she to know, if her husband didn't tell her anything?

He looked at her. "Kendall, you're going to have to go back to Hell's Colony."

She blinked. "Why?"

"Because I don't want you or my children around

here right now. None of the other wives are at Rancho Diablo. Certainly not the kids."

She looked at him, wishing he wasn't so handsome, wishing she didn't like him so much. Like? Try falling in love. "I'm not going."

He raised a brow. "It's been suggested that my attention is too divided with you around. That I'm not focused on my job."

"Focus harder." She peered into his face, not understanding why he was so angry. "I do my job. You can do yours. I'm not leaving my husband."

His lips went flat.

"Guess this is our first disagreement as man and wife," she said. "Kind of stinks, since it's also our first date."

He sighed. "Kendall. I can't keep an eye on you every second."

"That's right. And you shouldn't try. I'm going to do what I want to do." She laid her menu down, put her hand over his. "Is this because I talked to Storm?"

"You think I'm jealous?"

"Aren't you?"

"Hell, yeah." Sloan shook his head. "But it's not why you need to leave Rancho Diablo. It wasn't a wolf or a bear, or whatever excuse you gave, that attacked you. However you justified it. It was someone who was trying to kidnap you, most likely to use you to get information about Molly and Jeremiah Callahan. As long as you're here, you'll be a target. Our children…can you imagine how you'd feel if one of the babies was taken?"

She wasn't going to answer that. She was only three months along, maybe. The babies wouldn't be arriving for months.

But she could tell by the look on his face that he really didn't want her in Diablo. "Sloan."

He took her hands in his. "Babe. You've got to go to Hell's Colony."

Tears pricked her eyes, but she wouldn't cry. Wouldn't admit how much it hurt. "Okay."

"Thank you." His hands slipped away, and he leaned back. "I'll relax knowing you're safe."

"No, you won't. You never relax." She put her napkin on the table. "I'm going back to the ranch."

"Hang on. I'll take you."

She couldn't face a silent ride home. "I'll wait outside."

She could see Sloan's dilemma. But if they didn't spend time with each other now, when would they ever really become close? Their lives were so very different.

She stood outside the restaurant, wishing she'd worn her comfortable footwear instead of the stiletto, black suede boots she'd chosen in an attempt to look sexy for her husband. It was like trying to romance a stone.

"Excuse me," someone said, and she looked up to see two women smiling at her from a dark green truck. Snow fell, dusting the pavement and the vehicle's roof. "Can you give us directions to—"

But she didn't hear the rest. Suddenly she was hustled into a truck that pulled up behind the green one, and both vehicles sped away. Kendall pushed hard against the door, trying to escape, but her hands were swiftly tied and tape placed over her mouth though she desperately twisted her head to avoid it.

A hood dropped over her head and someone buckled a seat belt over her.

Then there was silence—except for the sound of Kendall's heart pounding hard, practically thundering. She felt a little faint, hoped she didn't get a wave of nausea. The smelly duct tape pulled at her mouth.

Someone was going to get an earful when she finally got this tape off.

KENDALL WAS TAKEN from the truck not long later, and walked through snow farther than she wanted to in her stiletto boots. When the hood was finally removed, she saw she was in a cave. A dark-haired female removed the tape from her mouth while someone untied her wrists, and a tough-eyed older man who would have been handsome if he wasn't a criminal stepped close to her.

Kendall slapped him with all her might. "You jerk," she said. "Do you know what you've done? Do you have any idea who I am?"

He rubbed his face, then motioned for the two females accompanying him to back away. "You're a Callahan woman. That's all I need to know."

She was furious. "My name is Kendall Phillips. I have three brothers, all trained to kill." She fibbed a bit about Xav, but who knew what the Callahans had been teaching him since he'd been on the ranch? Anyway, the story made her feel stronger. "They all have bad tempers, I assure you—tempers they inherited from our father, Gil Phillips. We own the largest manufacturing company for heavy machinery in the world. That's right," she said, barely taking a breath, "*that* Phillips. And my absence will not go unnoticed long, since my job is my life. Or was my life. If you kidnapped me because of my husband, let me tell you about him. He has a *very* bad temper. And he's grouchy and possessive. Bad move on your part. He has five brothers, and I'm pretty sure they're all trained to do something harmful to the human body. And you don't even want to know about their sister." Kendall glanced at the two females in the cave. "You girls just think you're tough. For your sake, I hope it's not my sister-in-law who comes for me, because I'm pretty sure even her brothers are afraid of her. This is the worst day of your life," she told the man listening to her rant. "And you've ruined my best Manolo Blahnik boots, you ape," she finished.

"That's interesting," he said. "Thanks for the warning. Tell me something. All these people you mention—are they living at Rancho Diablo?"

She looked at him. "Isn't that why you took me? Because you think you can find out something about the Callahans?"

"Maybe." He smiled. She noticed his scar and his broken nose, thinking that when he was younger he'd probably been very attractive except that he was a creepy jerk. "If your husband is at Rancho Diablo, then where are the other Callahans?"

She shook her head. "I have no idea. That's information above my pay grade, to quote my husband."

Her captor looked at her. "If your name is Kendall Phillips, what's your husband's name?"

"What's yours?" Kendall asked, figuring she might as well stall, give Sloan a chance to find her.

"You're my guest," the man reminded her. "You go first."

She looked around the cold cave. "Some host."

"Name."

"Sloan," she said, seeing no reason not to tell him.

"Ah. Sloan Chacon." He smiled again. "I know him well."

"I doubt it." She glared at him. "He doesn't let anybody know him well." Kendall was too angry to hold her tongue. A lightning flash of intuition hit her: Sloan had mentioned three mercenaries were supposedly living in the canyons. The Callahans would have been looking for three men.

But maybe it was one man and two women.

She decided to continue talking, see if she could learn anything Sloan could use. "What's interesting is how lucky you are that I didn't get any morning sickness while you had that nasty tape on my mouth."

"Morning sickness?" He frowned at her.

"I'm pregnant," she said, and he drew back. "With twins," she added, liberally revealing information that her captors couldn't find appealing. "I get lots of cravings. And lots of morning sickness. I vomit *a lot.* And it's always projectile."

"Oh, *great,*" one of the women said.

Her hulking captor looked at her, assessing her story, weighing his options. Kendall figured Sloan would probably be here in about five minutes, knowing him, and all hell would break loose.

"You're going to be more trouble than you're worth," he said.

"Tough mistake in your line of work," Kendall said, feeling pretty cheerful about that.

He jerked his head at the women. "Take her back."

"She's seen us," the dark-haired one said.

"True." He nodded. Then he spoke in a language Kendall didn't recognize, and once more the hood dropped over her face.

The adrenaline wore off, and fear took its place.

SLOAN WAS ANNOYED.

When he was with Kendall, he experienced that emotion frequently. He looked around outside the restaurant, trying to figure out where she might have gone. She could have met someone she knew and wanted to chat with. He could have missed her in the restaurant. Possibly she'd simply gotten upset with him and left.

She would never do that.

He tugged his collar up around his neck and waited. It was all he could do, and the feeling was novel—and unpleasant. He wasn't a very patient person.

"Hey."

He looked at the elderly woman who appeared beside him on the sidewalk.

"Hello," he answered politely.

"If you're looking for a blonde about medium height, she got into a truck with some people."

He looked over the woman, checking her eyes for honesty and her demeanor for duplicity. It was possible she was lying, but he didn't think so. Her blue eyes were clear and earnest.

"How do you know she was with me?" he asked.

She shrugged, her cherry-red coat pulling tight over her generous frame. "You look like you're waiting for someone. She was a really pretty lady, looked like she was dressed up for a date. And not too happy to leave with the people she went with. But if she wasn't with you, then—"

"Wait." He put a hand on the woman's arm to stop her. "How many people? What were they driving?"

"Dark green truck, followed by a tan truck that looked like it was used for off-roading. Mud smeared on the license plate."

His radar went on high alert. "How long ago?"

"Ten minutes." She cocked her head. "It was dark, so I couldn't see more than that." She shrugged. "Sorry I can't be more help. Tell Fiona I said hello."

He looked at her. "You know Aunt Fiona?"

She smiled. "Everyone knows your aunt Fiona. We've been best friends for years. Tell her Corinne Abernathy said it's time for a meeting of the Books'n'Bingo Society."

"Yes, ma'am," Sloan said, trying not to be rude and dash off, but panic was rising inside him. "Thank you, ma'am."

"If it helps, they went that way," Corinne said, pointing.

Sloan touched his hat and ran to his truck, dialing Galen with fingers that hadn't been this unsteady since the night he'd fired at his first target on the other side of the world.

KENDALL TRIED NOT TO panic, even though she was cold and frightened. They'd taken her boots—she'd protested, but apparently even thuggy-looking girls dug great boots—and gave her a yucky pair of old tennis shoes, which were not the least bit fashionable. She didn't even want to think about the disgusting things on her feet now.

Sloan would be here any minute.

What had they been fighting about at dinner? She couldn't remember. It was no longer important. As soon as she saw him, she was going to kiss him like he'd never been kissed before.

Time crawled, and then the truck stopped. The door opened.

"Get out," one of the horrible women said.

"I can't see." Obviously.

Someone dragged her from the truck. Doors slammed, an engine roared and she heard the vehicle drive away.

After a moment, Kendall realized she was alone.

With her hands tied and a hood on her head. She bent over, shaking the hood to the ground.

"I have no idea where I am," she muttered, looking around at the frozen landscape. "Sloan, this is a good time for the cavalry to arrive."

But maybe the cavalry wouldn't. So she had to get her wrists untied. She was miles from anything she recognized, surrounded by snow-lined canyons. Thready gray clouds streaked the dark sky. If it snowed again, her tracks would be covered. She was wearing tennis shoes, and already the snow was seeping in through the thin canvas.

She had her babies to think of. Her freezing to death or getting pneumonia was not going to do them a whole lot of good, so she was going to have to figure this out herself.

Kendall tugged on the plastic tie on her wrists with her teeth, thankful her hands were in front of her. To her surprise, the plastic popped free.

"On to civilization." She headed in the direction the truck had gone, stepping in the tire tracks. This road led somewhere, and if she told herself she was simply taking a nice, healthy walk for her babies, maybe she wouldn't panic about getting lost.

IT WASN'T DIFFICULT to follow the trucks that had taken Kendall. Sloan knew there had to be a connection to the hired guns in the canyons, and he knew they'd been waiting, watching, in order to have grabbed her from the sidewalk. So they weren't very far off.

He and his family fanned out in a deliberate pattern, searching for tracks. An hour later, Ash had located two sets of tire tracks in the snow near an outcropping.

She stared down at some tiny marks peppering the white snow. "Is she wearing high heels again?"

Sloan grunted, his stomach tight.

"They left," Galen said. "So either they've taken her somewhere else or they abandoned their plan."

"Follow that set of prints," Falcon said. "It's freshest. The rest of us will break up here."

Sloan took off in his truck, his heart thundering. Just when he thought he'd lost the trail, the tracks disappearing onto a two-lane, little-used road, Sloan saw two vehicles fitting Corinne's description heading westward. He called his brothers to warn them, then for some reason kept driving on. Why would they come back this way? Where had they gone?

His brothers and Ash would take care of the vehicles. He decided to see where this road led.

Twenty minutes later, that intuition led him to his wife, walking along the side of the road, with no purse, no boots, and obviously in high temper.

He stopped the truck and jumped out, and before he could get to Kendall, she'd launched herself into his arms.

"I knew you'd come," she whispered against his neck.

Sloan closed his eyes. This time he'd found her. Next time he might not be so lucky.

"Never seen you in a pair of tennis shoes," he murmured against her hair.

"They took my boots," she said, and then she kissed him, so desperately Sloan could only hold her tight.

"It's okay," he said. "We can get you more boots."

"It's not okay," she said, "it's the principle. It's personal now."

She kissed him so wildly Sloan almost didn't connect the dots. "Wait," he said, carrying her over to the truck. She was shivering, and he wanted to get her warm. "What does that mean, exactly?"

She pulled the offending tennis shoes off her feet with disgust. "It means," Kendall said, "that they could have hurt my children. When you catch those people, I'm getting my boots back."

Sloan looked at his determined wife. "What am I missing?"

"I wore those boots for you. I was trying to be beautiful for you."

He smiled. "I'm not too into the packaging. I'm kind of into the girl."

She sniffed, checked her face in the mirror. "You'd have to be a woman to understand. I'm going to smack those silly girls when you catch them. Once for my boots, and then once for each of my babies."

He laughed, then stopped. "Girls?"

"Two girls, one man."

Just as Corinne Abernathy had said. "Whoever's trying to take down my cousins sent women to do the job this time?"

His wife turned to look at him. "Can you think of any better way to get the job done?"

She had a helluva point.

"Sloan, I'm afraid I made a tactical error. I told them the Callahans were gone. They didn't seem to know that."

They'd been careful to spirit his cousins and their families out of town under cover of night so they couldn't be tracked. Sloan hesitated, not wanting to upset his wife more than she was already. All this talk of boots and vengeance worried him. "So they know we're not Jeremiah and Molly's family?"

She nodded. "I'm so sorry, Sloan. I realized I'd made a horrible mistake when their leader guy seemed so interested."

"Leader guy?"

"Big man. In charge. He called you Sloan Chacon. Said he knew you well, but I told him I didn't think so."

Sloan felt Kendall's gaze on him.

"Spoke a foreign language I've never heard before, and I've got a pretty good ear for languages," she added. "I do business around the world. I'm pretty familiar with accents."

He spoke a few sentences, and her eyes went wide. "That's it! How did you know?"

"I know," Sloan said grimly, "because sending family to hunt down family is the obvious thing to do."

KENDALL KNEW SHE'D MADE a mistake by running off at the mouth. She lay in the bed that night staring up in the dark, seeing nothing, hearing Sloan's even breathing beside her. He wasn't asleep. He insisted on staying with her—which gave her hope—yet it seemed they were further apart than ever. It wasn't that he didn't kiss her good-night, or that he didn't say anything except good-night once he got in bed.

She might as well be in Hell's Colony.

"I made a terrible mistake, didn't I?"

He didn't reply. But she heard a deep sigh.

She rolled over, put her head on his shoulder. "I'm so sorry, Sloan."

He stroked her back. "I'm glad you're all right."

"I didn't tell him where the family is."

She felt him tense. "Did he ask?"

"He did. I told him I had no idea. He seemed to believe me."

Silence. Kendall felt her heart breaking. Even though Sloan wouldn't admit it, she knew she'd made a tragic error. Maybe jeopardized everyone's safety. There was only one thing she could do.

"Sloan?"

"Mmm?"

"Remember when you said that it would be best if I went back to Hell's Colony so you could concentrate on what needs to be done here?"

"Yeah." His arm fell away from her.

"I think I'll go home tomorrow."

After a long moment, Sloan said, "That's a good plan."

And he didn't say anything else—which was all Kendall needed to know.

Chapter Thirteen

The babies were born six months later, on a warm July day when Kendall no longer thought about the frightening night in the frozen canyons. Two baby boys were placed in her arms, and it was such an amazing moment—so perfect in every way—that the only thing missing was Sloan.

She'd heard very little from her husband since she'd left. Living in Hell's Colony was so much a world away from Rancho Diablo that Kendall missed him all the time.

At the same time, she'd known what their marriage was from the very beginning: temporary.

"He's going to love you," she told her sons. "You'll be proud that you have such a big, strong daddy."

Jonas came into the nursery to examine his nephews. "Always amazes me that such tiny things grow up to be cowboys, and putty for the fairer sex."

Kendall smiled. "Sounds like a man who loves his family."

"Yeah." He sat on a blue-cushioned rocker. "Does Sloan know?"

She nodded. "We don't talk much. He doesn't want me…me being tracked here." Kendall hated to admit it, but maybe it was time. "When I was kidnapped, I made the mistake of revealing that all of you had gone." It felt good to get the confession off her chest. "Jonas, I'm so sorry."

"If it hasn't mattered in six months, nothing's going to change now," he said, and Kendall knew he was trying to make her feel better.

"The thing is, if the people who want to find your parents can locate me, they can track you."

"I know. Sloan told me everything. Don't worry about it." Jonas unwrapped a blue cigar from a candy bouquet and munched on it. "What did you name them?"

Kendall looked at her sleeping boys. They were wrapped in little white T-shirts, and wore tiny white socks with blue stripes on their feet. "Carlos Gilchrist Chacon Callahan and Isaiah Sloan Chacon Callahan."

Jonas smiled. "Impressive handles for them to grow into."

She nodded, feeling horrible about endangering her friends. "How's the bunkhouse?"

"Going up. Looks great. After the harsh winter we had, things got slowed down quite a bit. But your detailed notes and plans have kept the project moving smoothly."

"You're trying to make me feel better."

"That's something I never do, waste words on employees to make them feel better."

She needed to hear that. Was glad to know her work was valued. Yet it had been easy for her to become a liability. "I have a flat in Paris."

"We don't have to go anywhere, Kendall," Jonas said. "This place is a compound. The wives and kids are safer here than just about anyplace. Plus the security is beefed up. Eventually, our friends are going to slip up, and your husband and my cousins are going to be on the bad guys like stink on horse crap. Quit worrying so much."

"I'm going to Paris," Kendall said. "I can work from there."

"There's no reason to do that," Jonas said. "They're not going to find you here, Kendall."

She wasn't worried about being found. "If I'd left when Sloan asked me to, none of this would have happened. But I was stubborn, I thought I knew best. I wanted to get to know my husband," she told Jonas, "but I didn't realize how much was at stake. My children. Your children."

"Kendall." Jonas chomped on the candy cigar. "Go if you think you must. But just know that nothing bad is going to happen to any of us. You didn't give up any information that they wouldn't have figured out eventually. They're mercs for a reason."

But they knew she was having twins. She'd told them the company name, had bragged about her brothers. No doubt they were already having the Phillips compound watched. Of course they were. They'd been trying to get at the Callahans for years, and this place was a lot easier to stake out than miles of hard, winding canyons.

"Jonas, they know where you are."

"I know. It doesn't matter."

"It does to me. As much as I hated being kidnapped, at least it was just me. It would kill me if it was one of the children." She glanced toward her precious sons. "I always swore up and down I was simply a career woman. But now I have them," she said, tears gathering in her eyes, "and I realize exactly how much damage I've done to your family."

He broke the blue candy cigar in half and handed her a piece. "Kendall, they were going to find us eventually. We were always prepared for that. Being in your compound bought us time. Those hired guns will never be successful. And that's not just bravado talking. We don't know where our parents are, we don't know where Sloan's parents are. The mercs can wait out there until they're a hundred years old and they'll never find them. There are some things that can never be found."

THE BROTHERS SAT in the upstairs library, celebrating the good news that had been passed on by Jonas Callahan.

"Two sons," Falcon said. "That's awesome, bro." He high-fived his brother.

Galen studied the photos Jonas had texted over. "They don't look a thing like you, thank God. It's all their mother's genes. For which we are grateful."

Guffaws met that comment. Sloan grinned, prouder than he'd ever been. "They do look like their mother." He missed Kendall terribly, would probably never get over the soft feel of her skin, the gentleness of her touch, the taste of her lips. There was only so much a man could think about without going mad.

He'd known a lot of emotional pain in his life, but a lot of happy times, too. The birth of his boys by a woman he knew he'd fallen in love with brought on a mixture of those emotions.

"Are you going to see them?" Ash asked.

No one in the room said anything. It was a question born of hope, but one they all knew the answer to. The thought that his offspring could ever be kidnapped punched fear into him. He considered himself a fairly strong man, but that would bring him to his knees. His sons—or any Callahan child or wife—were why he and his siblings were here. To make sure that never happened.

He raised a glass to his brothers and sister. "Thanks for celebrating the happy occasion with me."

"So now what?" Jace asked.

Now…now they'd probably get a divorce one day. No marriage survived time that stretched but never ended, and he and Kendall wouldn't be able to spend time together like a normal married couple for a long time. If ever.

But he'd known all along that he wasn't the kind of man she would have chosen, if circumstances hadn't conspired to bring them together. "I don't know what happens now," Sloan said, even though he did.

It just hurt too damn much to talk about.

FIONA WENT OUT in the sunshine to look at the strands of red, white and blue lights strung along the fence. She loved to decorate as much as she loved to bake, but it hadn't been as much fun to put out the pretty lights for Independence Day without all the children around to gaze at them with delight. There'd been no fireworks, either, and she couldn't remember a time when there hadn't been fireworks at Rancho Diablo. It was a family tradition, one even the folks in the town of Diablo came out to enjoy.

She sighed, wishing she could go visit Kendall's new babies. Jonas had sent her a photo by text, but it wasn't the same as holding a baby. There was nothing like the powdery-fresh fragrance of a sweet, precious baby. And she just knew Kendall needed her help. Kendall had been pretty much confined to bed and rocker for the last three months of her pregnancy. The babies had been born just past preemie, so that had been good, and Fiona knew there were a ton of Callahan wives and menfolk around that would help her. For that matter, there was plenty of staff in the Hell's Colony compound, so Kendall lacked for nothing.

But Fiona was missing out on being part of the babies' lives. And she missed her grand-nieces and grand-nephews more than her old heart could stand, or at least it felt like it.

She began to remove the lights from the corral posts, tugging at the strand and unwinding it, sunk in her thoughts. Maybe a visit to her friends at the Books'n'Bingo tearoom and bookshop would cheer her up.

But she doubted it. She just felt so rudderless without all the children around. Raising Jonas and his brothers had been some of the happiest times of her life. Even when the boys had been up to their necks in mischief, she'd been happy. In fact, maybe she'd enjoyed those times the most mainly because the trouble they'd gotten into hadn't been bad, just basic boy hijinks.

She'd loved raising her sister's children, even if she'd always wished Molly and Jeremiah could have been around themselves. Without children of her own, she'd felt needed by the boys she and Burke had raised.

She'd asked Burke if they could journey out to see the new babies, and visit with the other children, but he had said no, he didn't think so. Ashlyn had told him that they'd found marks of a dead campfire in the canyons, and they didn't think it was from random travelers moving across the ranch.

So they were being cautious.

But Fiona was going stir-crazy. And she wanted children around.

Chief Running Bear appeared at her side. "Let's talk."

She glanced around, rolled the lights into a ball she set on a post. "I've got cookies. Come inside. It's safer."

"You seem sad," he said, following her.

"I miss babies."

He laughed, and she shook her head. "A happy home has movement and laughter in it."

She handed him the cookie tray, and he took a chocolate chip, one of his favorite things she baked. "You are worried."

"Yes, old friend, I am." Fiona sighed. "We ask a lot of these new Callahans. And Jonas's family are all settled happily in Tempest, at Dark Diablo, and in Hell's Colony. The children love their schools. I'm afraid they'll never return here."

He sat down, munched his cookie, accepted the hot black coffee she poured for him. He wouldn't drink iced tea—only coffee. "Life has changed."

"Will it be this way forever?" Fiona asked, her heart aching.

"Until it's over. But think of it this way. They won't find Jeremiah and Molly. They'll never find Carlos and Julia. Both sides of the family are safe."

"So these boys'—and Ash's—parents are alive?"

The chief nodded. "Galen knows where they are. But he will never tell."

Fiona blinked. "Why does he know?"

"He's eldest. He had to be told—he was pulled out of medical school to take care of his siblings."

"I don't understand."

"Galen had graduated from college and was just

starting med school many years ago, when Jeremiah and Molly went into witness protection and we told Jonas and the boys their parents had gone to heaven. Julia and Carlos continued their work. Julia was CIA, and had access to information that could have been helpful to us, if we'd needed it. Unfortunately, they realized that in order to continue the work Jeremiah and Molly had done, it was best they go into hiding, as well. This kept their children safe."

"What a terrible burden for Galen," Fiona said. "He could have only been twenty-three or so."

"He did eventually return to medical school once all the siblings had reached eighteen, but yes." The chief sipped his coffee. "Everyone made sacrifices, even you. To keep all the children safe."

Fiona rarely ate the cookies she baked, but today felt she needed extra fortification. She stirred some whiskey into her coffee, offered some to the chief, who declined. "But the rest of the boys—Sloan and the others—they don't know their parents are alive?"

"Yes, they do. They know they had to go away. But the tribe helped guide them, raise them. Taught them the sacred ways. It was not a bad way to grow up, Fiona. It prepared them."

"But still." She shook her head. "What do they get for protecting us? Protecting the land and the Diablos? And the children?"

"What do you want them to have?"

"Children," Fiona said, her voice a whisper. "Their childhood back, through their own children. So that they can know the happiness family brings."

He put a hand over hers briefly. "You worry too much, my friend. They are happy."

"They can't be. Sloan can't even see his new babies.

Their names are Carlos and Isaiah." Fiona sighed. "He doesn't say it, but I know he misses Kendall."

"He's a soldier. He'll do what he has to do."

"It's not fair," Fiona said angrily. "I hate those evil people out there! They're taking my family's lives away!"

"Not their lives," the chief said.

"I know. And I'm grateful for that. I meant they're taking the most important things in life away from them. My wish for them is that each of these Callahans—Carlos and Julia's family—find happiness with someone they love."

"We did it before," he reminded her. "You didn't think you'd ever get your nephews to the altar."

She smiled, wiped her tears with a tissue. "What are you suggesting?"

"To help them."

"I'm listening."

"On the other side of the canyons there are twenty thousand acres that have gone up for sale. I know the man who owns the land. I also know that the mercenaries hide in the canyons and camp up there."

Fiona studied her friend and companion. "Go on."

"We have plenty of silver between us, you and I. We can buy the land, deed it to Rancho Diablo. Award it in five years to the one with the desire to live there."

She stared. "What if they all want to live there?"

"Probably that won't happen. This is a job for them, like any other assignment they would have been sent on."

"But still. What if?"

"They have to be married for the chance to win it."

"The *chance?*" she asked.

"Just a chance. A one in seven chance."

"But what if they can't find someone they want to marry in five years?" Fiona asked. "I hear rumors that Sloan and Kendall will get divorced soon."

He considered that. "It can't happen."

"It can when two people never live together and never have the chance to know each other. I don't care what you say, family sticks together."

"Then that's it." He looked satisfied. "They have to be married, and settled on the land across the canyons, with children, most importantly."

"And if they all want it?" she asked again. "It could happen."

"More like none of them will," the chief said. "Tighe and Dante love the rodeo. Ash is young—she doesn't want to settle down. It would take a brave man to show her that she wants a union. Falcon is a seeker. He'll never settle in one place. Already he's chafing, being here. Jace doesn't know what he wants, but he remembers the good times and thinks he just wants to go back to the tribe. Galen has had the weight of responsibility for so long, I don't know that he'll ever care to settle down. You had to have been as surprised as I was that Sloan married. He is a seeker, too, but still a loner."

"I don't know what to think anymore. What if they don't want the land? What if they don't even want to be here, now? I wouldn't if I was them."

"They're aware of the danger, and realize they have special training that is helpful." Chief Running Bear put his coffee down. "They will always stand for family."

"But they don't know us. They have to give up their hopes and dreams to stay here for so long."

"They know what family is," he told her. "And in the tribe, family is important. It's everything."

"All right. Buy the land," Fiona said. "Put it under

the business auspices of Rancho Diablo. You tell the boys and Ashlyn what we want to do for them."

"They will not thank you," the chief warned. "Settling down is not in their nature. This is a carrot for the horse, but a horse doesn't always want the carrot if he doesn't trust the man offering."

"Rancho Diablo is my heart," Fiona said with warmth. "This is where my sister's family grew up. I don't want them to be here unless they wish to be."

"They will understand this land in time. And it's the best way to keep the family together."

"And safe." Fiona pondered the idea. "Thank you for thinking of it."

"Again, they will not necessarily thank you," he said, putting on a straw cowboy hat over his long, braided hair. "The wild horse never thanks the lasso."

"And the mercs who are living on the land now?"

"Will be in for a surprise. We'll have them trapped on all sides. And the Diablos will always be free." The chief went out the door, disappearing the way he always did, with hardly a sound.

Or they'd be building their own trap. Fiona went back to pulling down the Independence Day lights, hoping that this time next year, there'd be lots of children back on the ranch to enjoy them, if the chief's idea worked. She wasn't so sure.

But maybe there'd be no need to force Carlos and Julia's family to stay here if they didn't want to. Surely something would happen to change the course of Callahan destiny.

Chapter Fourteen

Kendall awakened with a jerk and realized someone was sitting on the foot of her bed, looking down into the babies' bassinets. "Sloan?"

"Yeah."

"You came!"

He put a hand over hers. "Hellfire couldn't keep me from you and the babies."

She moved to sit beside him. "Aren't they amazing?"

"They're beautiful. I wish I could have been with you when they were born." He looked sad about that.

"You're here now." She touched his shoulder, astonished that it felt as if they hadn't been apart as long as they had. It had been too long. She wished it could be the way it had been once between them, before she'd given away the location of the Callahans.

"I told my brothers and Ash that I was leaving now that you were home from the hospital." He reached one finger out to delicately caress the baby nearest him. "I can't believe I'm actually a father." He turned to look at her, and she saw the emotion in his eyes, in the glow of the night-light she left on so she could tend to the babies. "It would kill me if something happened to one of these little miracles."

She smiled. "Carlos and Isaiah are going to love their daddy."

He looked back at his sons. "Carlos and Isaiah. My boys. *Our* boys."

"How long are you staying?" Kendall asked, almost afraid to hear the answer.

"Not long. Two days. We've seen more activity lately, so something may be up. They couldn't do much during the hard winter we had, so they'll try to maximize their summer opportunities."

Sloan crawled into bed with Kendall, and after a long, hesitant moment, she molded herself against his chest. It felt as if he'd come home. Kendall was his home, and Sloan, who'd never wanted to be tied to one hearth, wanted to be with her forever.

He didn't know how to tell her what he had to say. It was going to rip his heart out.

"Sloan?"

"Yeah?"

"I missed you."

He smiled in the darkness. "The only way I kept moving every day was knowing that you were here, safe."

But it had still been hell.

"I wouldn't have ever let you go if you hadn't been taken that day."

She raised her head to look at him. "You wouldn't have?"

"No. No man lets his wife go." He tightened his arm around her waist as she lay back down. "I just knew the babies were safer here."

But the future hung between them, a silent question.

"Now what?" Kendall asked softly.

"It will be over one day."

She looked at him. "And then?"

He kissed her. "Then we'll figure out the future."

She sighed. "I wasn't going to bring this up now, but given that you might disappear, and since the babies are being quiet for an astonishingly generous length of time, this may be my only chance." She put a gentle hand against his cheek. "I want to go back with you."

What man didn't want to hear that his woman wanted to be with him?

"You're a brave woman, Kendall Callahan."

"You're a hot husband. I intend to be with my man."

He kissed her hand. "It's too dangerous for the babies. One day they'll be strapping young men, but right now they're pretty little."

"The boys have a bodyguard. I called Ash today. She said she'd be happy to do the honors."

He looked down at his little wife, not entirely surprised that she'd been maneuvering to get what she wanted. "Ash's post is Fiona and Burke."

"She always says she's getting fat. She won't get fat bodyguarding us," Kendall said. "We get maybe two hours of sleep a night, uninterrupted. And Falcon says he'll be happy to teach me how to fire my gun better. Says by the time he gets done coaching me, I'll be able to hit the needles off a cactus at fifty paces."

Sloan chuckled. "I missed the hell out of you. The hardest thing I've ever done was not be with my wife and children. You say I'm a loner, but my wife and boys can give me all the social time they want to."

"Do you mean it?"

"Yeah." He nodded. "It's probably not wise, but I do believe I can keep you and the boys safe. And with Ash on point, my sons couldn't have a better champion. But not for a while."

"I promise not to do anything that's unsafe."

"I know. Of course, just walking outside a restaurant shouldn't have been unsafe." In fact, taking her and the boys home with him would be like poking his finger in the eye of the devil. But he was a selfish man. He wanted his wife, and he definitely wanted to know his babies. He'd brave the gates of hell to be a father to his precious sons.

It was too painful. He knew what it felt like to be deserted by one's parents.

"Don't remind me of that night." She studied his eyes. "Did you ever find out who kidnapped me?"

He didn't want to tell her. Had hoped she wouldn't ask. "It's not going to make you feel any better."

"I'm not a woman who dwells a lot in fear, Sloan."

"We believe the man who took you that night is a CIA operative who knew my mother when she was in the agency." He didn't want to say more, but Kendall had the right to know what she'd married into. "From your description, we believe he is our father's brother."

"There were three brothers? Jeremiah, Carlos and another?"

He nodded. "The black sheep of the family, you might say. The rogue agent, Wolf."

"So he knows all your secrets. Because he's part of the family."

Sloan nodded. "He has a greater ability to find Molly and Jeremiah. So you were a natural target, and would be still."

She ignored that. "Does Jonas know that you think it's his uncle who's trying to bring him down?"

He hadn't told his cousin. The person they needed to talk to was their grandfather. "I will, now that I know for sure who it was."

"Do you know for certain? My description could have been—"

"Falcon was able to verify that Wolf is on the move again."

"Who were the women with him? The ones that stole my boots?"

He smiled. "You're still annoyed about that, aren't you?"

"It wasn't the boots so much as it became personal. If they'd take me, and then my clothes, where would they draw the line?" She touched the lightning-strike tattoo on the back of Sloan's shoulder, running her finger down it. "If they'd asked, I would have gladly given them the stupid boots. I'd just never had anyone *take* something from me. In business, people generally negotiate for what they want. Anyway, the stupid boots were a bit too small and pinched my feet a little, so it wasn't a great loss."

"Why did you buy them if they were too small?" He kissed her nose.

She smiled, looking like a mischievous little girl, which entranced him. "I'd seen them on the runway in Paris. The one size they had left was the size I bought. And I was only wearing them that night because I was trying to be sexy for you."

He kissed her. "You're sexy barefoot."

"A girl can be vain, just a little." She traced his lip, then kissed him. "Who were the women with him?"

"We assume some kind of CIA operatives. It would make sense that Wolf would load his team with experts. They're not important." Sloan tucked her head under his chin. "Go to sleep while my sons are napping."

"I want it to be like it was before, Sloan."

He knew what Kendall was talking about. She meant

before she'd told Wolf that it was Chacon Callahans at Rancho Diablo, and that the Callahans they sought were long gone. She felt guilty, and he understood that. Everything had changed. He wasn't certain it could be put back together. This was his home, his family. He wanted to be with them, whatever the cost.

He hadn't been completely honest with his wife. She could come back to Rancho Diablo—but not until the coast was clear. He hadn't wanted to mar their time together by telling her so, but he would never risk Kendall, or his children.

He needed her too much. Even if she didn't believe that he did.

IN THE NIGHT, the boys woke up, making little noises that Sloan felt deep in his heart. They were so helpless, so defenseless. He loved them so much. His world had always been dark and secretive, but these babies were lightness and life to him. As was Kendall. What could he say? He'd protect them with all he had.

"Come here," he told Carlos, picking him up to cradle him against his chest. "I don't know much about what babies want, but I'm a fast learner."

Kendall rolled over. "Hand him to me, Sloan."

He did, gently caressing the tender baby skin as he held out his son. "He's as strong as you are."

"You're a romantic," Kendall said, and she sounded surprised. "Thank you, Sloan."

"You don't think I have a romantic side?" Sloan asked gruffly.

She smiled, and he felt stronger. "You're very romantic."

Another baby noise caught his attention. "Hey, little

one." He picked up Isaiah. "Mom's taking care of your brother right now. You're going to have to talk to me."

"There's a bottle in the fridge over there. You can run it under some warm water to knock the chill off, if you want to feed him."

"All right. Come on, little man." He warmed the bottle, then sat in a rocker, amazed that his son took to the bottle as if he was used to his father feeding him. "We make a good team," he told him, his heart twisting when a little hand wrapped around his finger.

Isaiah kept drinking, his trusting eyes looking up at him, stealing inside him. "Your brother's luckier than you. He got the breast."

Kendall giggled. "Sloan, that's breast milk you're feeding him."

"But he's not getting it from a breast. If I was a baby, you can bet I'd rather have the breast than a bottle." Sloan thought about that. "You have beautiful breasts."

"You haven't seen them in months. And they've changed."

He smiled. "Ask any man whose wife has had his children if he thinks her breasts have changed, and I bet his answer is that his wife's breasts are more beautiful now."

"If you keep saying those sweet things, you're going to make me cry."

He looked down at Isaiah. He stopped sucking for a moment, then started again. "I don't want to make you cry. I want to make you happy."

"You do." She smiled at him. "So much."

He got up, crossed to the bed, settled next to her with Isaiah in his arms. "I'm glad the babies look like you."

"They don't really look like anyone right now. But when they finally do, I'm kind of hoping they'll have your dark hair. And your smile. Those navy eyes that are a sure Callahan mark."

"Did you name Carlos for my father?" he asked.

"I did."

They didn't talk anymore. Kendall took Isaiah when Sloan fell asleep with his baby son against his chest. She changed the infant, burped him and put him back in his bassinet, then changed Carlos. The baby let out an annoyed squawk at one point, and Kendall smiled, recognizing the signal. "You're more like your daddy than he realizes. But you probably got some stubbornness from your mother, too." She moved Carlos to the bassinet, putting him up against his brother. Both babies stopped squirming, settling immediately now that they were touching each other.

Kendall smiled at her sons. Then she got into bed next to Sloan. He rolled over, lining up against her back, burying his face against her neck before he lay still. At peace.

Kendall closed her eyes, her heart finally happy. Content.

Completely in love. Beyond a shadow of a doubt.

WHEN KENDALL WOKE UP, she saw Sloan standing over her. "Hello."

He looked at her. "I have to go back."

She nodded. "I know. I'm coming, too."

He caressed her face. "You are. But not now."

She got out of bed. "We're a family. We stay together."

"Kendall, the babies are less than a month old. They need to be here. You've got an army of staff. They have family to love them. I know that you're all safe here. Let's wait until they're a little older."

Kendall shook her head as if she didn't agree, but would go along with his wishes. "All right."

He crooked a brow at her. "No argument?"

"No," she said. "No argument."

"It won't be long."

"You'd let me and the boys come with you if I hadn't blown the cover of the operation."

"It doesn't matter anymore. There was no harm done."

She looked into his eyes, searching. "Sloan, it has to matter. Jonas says it doesn't, but I know it does."

She looked as if she might cry, and Sloan wanted to comfort her, but knew she was right. Trust had been broken, and so much might have been jeopardized. "Kendall—"

She turned away. "I understand why it's better if I stay here. It's safer for everyone. Not just the babies."

He nodded. "Everything's going to be all right."

"I know." She wiped her eyes and turned back around. "Thanks for coming to visit."

"I'll see you soon."

She nodded, and he left, already wishing he was back with Kendall and his boys.

"Okay," Fiona said, striding into the bunkhouse on a Sunday afternoon. It was a hot July day—steamy and windy enough to tease fires onto the baked land—and Sloan was feeling edgy. "We need to talk."

The men stood, and Ash patted the seat next to her. "Sit here, Aunt Fiona."

"I won't sit, thank you. This isn't a social visit. This is about the direction of the family. Sit, gentlemen, please."

They did, and Sloan knew why Fiona commanded

such respect in the town of Diablo. She was a virtual dynamo. Her white hair was pulled back tight from her face in a bun that never seemed to stay completely together. She had skin the color of pale milk sprinkled with cinnamon, and her eyes always sparkled. She looked like a woman who enjoyed living life to its fullest, meeting all challenges head-on.

"Your grandfather advised me to purchase land north of here, across the canyons. It came up for sale, and he knew the man involved. Felt he could get a reasonable deal, and that it was good land." She glanced around the room. "This way, the chief believes, we can put a pincer movement on our friends in the canyons."

"I don't have a problem with that," Sloan said. "It's a smart move."

She nodded. "Most importantly, it leaves the Diablo mustangs completely free. The importance of that cannot be understated, as you know. This is their home. We'll keep their land secure forever."

"We'll be stretched a bit thin," Falcon pointed out. "But the good thing is that the mercs are now trespassing on our land."

Fiona nodded. "Here's the situation. Land is valuable. We can't run it all ourselves, of course. I know none of you is interested in staying in one place for very long," she said, shrewdly not looking at any of them, even though Sloan was pretty certain he was watching a one-act play being performed by a veteran actress. "But if you were of a mind to ever settle down, the land would be available to you."

"How?" Jace asked. "I'd be interested. I've made no secret of the fact that I want a family. I don't want to be a tumbleweed forever."

That roused a laugh from his brothers.

"Jace, no one would have you," Tighe said.

"Don't talk to him like that," Ash said. "Of course someone would want you, Jace."

"Why wouldn't someone have me?" Jace demanded, annoyed.

"Because you have a new woman every week. And females tend to take exception to that," Dante pointed out.

"I haven't had a woman since I got here," Jace said. "It's been a good ten months. Long enough for Sloan to have children. *I* want a child."

Fiona cleared her throat. "Children do factor into this offer, of course. Your grandfather was very clear about that. The land will go to whichever of you are interested in having a family. No bachelor pads." She smiled. "It's not good to have lone wolves around. The sheep get nervous."

Sloan wasn't certain he understood all of that. Aunt Fiona's mind worked differently than other people's at times. "I have a family."

Fiona blinked. "You do."

"But you don't want to live here, Sloanie," Ash said. "You're the wild man."

"I'm not as wild as I used to be." He smiled, thinking about his sons. "Getting tamer all the time. And my boys are going to need some room to stretch their legs."

Laughter broke out in the room. Fiona remained serious, studying him. "The way it works is that there's enough land for all seven of you. But should one of you not marry and have children, that portion is forfeited. Easy as pie, I think."

"What about me?" Ash asked. "They'll all get married, and I'll be the only one without any land."

"Why?" Fiona asked.

"Because she's different," Sloan said. "Ash is our empath. Our shaman. She'll always blow in the wind. It's her home."

"Well," Fiona said, "your grandfather didn't mention that you were to be given any different opportunity than your brothers. He figured none of you would take him up on his offer, seeing as how this isn't your home. He knew you'd one day want to go back to the tribe."

"Not me," Dante said. "I'm hitting the rodeo circuit when our assignment here is done."

"Me, too," his twin said. "I'm doing nothing but ride bulls until I finally can't ride anymore."

Fiona pressed her lips together. Sloan thought she looked a bit flummoxed. "Galen?"

"I don't know," he said. "I've always been responsible for this crowd. I don't know if I want to be tied to one place anymore."

"Well, think it over. You have five years to decide."

Sloan thought their aunt looked a bit alarmed as he walked her to the door. "Then what happens if none of us opts to settle here?"

She smiled at him. "You forfeit. Naturally."

"I have a wife and children."

"You're already eligible, then, aren't you?"

He nodded. "Yes, ma'am."

"Are you ready for a home and a place of your own?" Her bright eyes studied him. "Or will you return to wherever you came from?"

He'd been living in a cabin, in a place so remote only his grandfather and family knew where to find him. He didn't even have a landline, cable or electricity, preferring fires and kerosene lamps.

He couldn't raise a family under those circumstances. He thought about Kendall's fabulous home.

He couldn't live like that, either. Just the thought of it made him feel vaguely rattled, somehow caged in. The Phillipses' compound was enormous, bigger than Rancho Diablo, which was huge.

"I don't know where I'll be, Aunt Fiona," he said.

She looked at him, a soft smile in her eyes. "You'll know someday. And when you do, you can decide if you want to be the one who gets the land, and raise your family there. You wouldn't want your brothers' families to have more than yours would, I imagine. Kendall can take care of the children on her own, of course, but every father wants to provide his best, doesn't he?"

He looked at her. "Are you coaching me?"

She smiled. "I just don't want you left out. Your siblings are very competitive. I favor all my nephews and my niece, but it's also my duty to try to help all of you make decisions that benefit you. No regrets."

He enveloped her in his arms. "You are a good aunt."

"I know." She sniffled against his chest. "I am."

"Unorthodox, maybe."

"Yes. Proud of it."

He laughed. "I'll take your counsel under advisement."

Yet how could he ask Kendall to live the way he'd be living for the foreseeable future?

Chapter Fifteen

At the same time Sloan heard the Diablos thundering through the canyons, he also saw a rider coming up the road, his tall horse easily recognizable even at a distance. Sloan turned toward the canyons, searching for the wild black mustangs. Like Jonas's peacocks, which strutted during the day at the front of the property, the Diablos were something special that set Rancho Diablo apart. The first time he'd heard them running, the sound had been unmistakable and stirring.

He turned to face Storm Cash as the neighbor neared.

"Callahan," Cash said.

"Storm," Sloan said. "What brings you around?"

"I've been having some vagrants camp on my property. Was wondering if you were having the same problem."

Sloan shook his head. "Not to my knowledge."

Storm leaned back in the saddle, glanced around.

"Looking for something?" he demanded.

Cash turned to look at him, his expression amused. "Haven't seen your wife around in a while."

"Why would you see her, anyway?" His annoyance level began to rise.

"Met her once before the new bunkhouse was framed. She said she was in charge of the project. Noticed she hadn't been around to check on it."

Sloan leaned a boot against a fence rail. "My wife is not your concern."

"I meant nothing by it. I was only asking after her health."

Sloan had to admit to himself that he simply didn't like the big rancher. He was the kind of hombre women would call handsome. But Sloan had never gotten over the suspicion that Cash had thrown that rock through the library window. And what fool asked after another man's wife? "What the hell do you want?"

"Just being neighborly."

"I don't want to be neighborly."

Cash nodded. "I've heard you're a loner. Clearly an unfriendly one at that."

"State your business and head on," Sloan said. "I've got horses to tend."

Cash sighed. "Heard in town you're a new dad. Brought a gift by for the babies. I have no children of my own." He handed over a small box, white with aqua-colored ribbons. Obviously, professionally gift-wrapped. "Congratulations on becoming a father."

Sloan scowled. "I don't want a gift."

"What harm is a baby gift between neighboring ranchers?"

Ash came to stand at Sloan's side. "Hi," she said to Storm.

He smiled, and Sloan's irritation reached fever pitch. The rancher extended his hand for Ash to shake, and Sloan was curious to see if his sister would pick up anything about their unwanted visitor.

She glanced at Sloan. "The guys need you in the barn, brother."

He nodded. "Be seeing you," he said to his unwanted visitor.

Sloan couldn't force himself to thank him for the gift. There was just something off about the man, and he couldn't put his finger on it.

"You're not really needed in the barn," Ash said when they were out of earshot. "I could see your head steaming all the way from the upstairs window. What is the matter with you?"

"I just don't like him."

She laced her arm through Sloan's. "You don't like anyone."

"I like everyone until they give me a reason not to." He headed to the barn, anyway. "Did you see his aura?"

"Blue," Ash said. "Nothing unusual."

It wasn't much of a tell. But Ash would have noticed if there was anything to be suspicious about. He couldn't say why he didn't trust Storm Cash, but he didn't. "Maybe I'm not used to somebody asking after my wife and bringing a gift."

"It's a baby gift, not flowers and a candy heart, bro." Ash smiled. "You are a jealous, jealous man."

He pulled up. "Is that what's wrong with me?"

She laid her head on his shoulder as they walked. "Partially."

"Don't spare me."

"I won't, brother dear. It's not my style."

Sloan smiled to himself. In a way, his sister reminded him so much of Kendall, another independent, free spirit.

He and Ash walked into the barn, which was quiet except for blowing fans oscillating overhead, and an occasional horse whinny. Their brothers sat around in worn chairs, mending tack and saddles.

"Storm Cash says he's had trespassers on his place." Sloan sat down to join them. Ash settled nearby, reaching up to pet a horse's nose that stretched over a stall door.

"If he's got trespassers, he needs to hire more help," Falcon said.

"I believe he was trying to warn us." Among neighbors Sloan cared for, the warning would have been appreciated. He set the baby gift on a table, staring at it. "Tighe. Dante. Go over and pay Cash a visit. Take a look around. See what he's working over there. We need to know, since his ranch flanks us to the west."

Tight and Dante left the barn. Falcon looked at Sloan. "What if Cash is on our side? What if those trespassers are the mercs? They may have realized they can stay on his land and not be detected. We keep a pretty tight eye on things around here, so we know our ranch is relatively safe. His is open land."

Sloan thought about the mystical Diablos he'd heard galloping, their spirits wild and free, a sure portent of things to come according to Running Bear. Maybe that had been the warning. He'd forgotten to ask Jonas how the spirits worked.

Of course, spirits were unpredictable. That was their prerogative.

"Hi," he heard a female voice say, and Ash jumped to her feet.

"Kendall!" Ash ran to throw her arms around her sister-in-law. "You brought the babies!"

Sloan's heart leaped—then sank. He was so glad to see the lights of his life. "You shouldn't be here, Kendall." He enveloped his family in his arms. "My God, I'm glad you're here with me."

She leaned up to kiss him. "I've missed you so much. And the boys are growing so fast. We need you, Sloan. We need to be with you."

"Let me hold my nephew," Ash said, taking Isaiah from Kendall's arms.

"I'll hold the other one, if you don't think he'll cry," Galen said.

"I'd cry if I was a baby and saw your face," Ash told him. "Grab the baby and quit being so scared, Galen."

Sloan held his wife. "You can't stay here. Just for the night. Maybe two."

Kendall stepped back from him. "Sloan Callahan, I've come to negotiate a deal with you."

His brothers and sister laughed. Sloan took note of the determined gleam in his wife's eye and prepared himself. "I'm listening."

"Either I stay here or you go back to Hell's Colony with me. Or we go somewhere else." She took a deep breath. "Or we get that divorce we agreed on. It's your choice. But I've had enough of our family being apart just because your family's running from ghosts."

It hit him that Kendall was right. He *was* afraid. Deeply afraid. There'd been times in the military when he'd been worried, scared, intimidated, even wild-eyed with anger. But this woman and two small boys had heated his emotions to a new, raw level. Kendall was fearless.

He'd been too afraid to be with her. To make his family his priority.

"You're right," he said, and his brothers and Ash drifted away. "We'll work it out."

She backed up. Wearing her sky-high, flamingo-pink heels, a lime-green business suit that skimmed her curves and a smile just for him. "I hope we do. Because we need to give our marriage a chance. And it can't wait forever."

He took a deep breath. "I can't leave here. I can't leave my family right now. I can't leave Fiona and Burke."

"I understand." She walked out of the barn.

He followed in a hurry. "Isaiah and Carlos shouldn't be here."

"I'm not putting them in danger." Kendall went to her Range Rover, began pulling out luggage. "When your family believed that you were too sidetracked by me to do your job, I left. But the bad guys don't want me, Sloan. I already gave away the secrets. So I figure there's nothing else that can go wrong now. Except my marriage." She handed him a couple of baby bags. "Can you carry those inside? Fiona says we're to have the upstairs master. The nursery's closer to it."

"Fiona?" He followed after his wife as she walked to the front of the house. "You've been talking to Aunt Fiona?"

"Fiona was the one who called and told me to come." Kendall gave Sloan a smile he could only classify as sexy and devious. "Be warned. I've brought assistance."

He realized a black Range Rover that matched Kendall's had pulled up behind hers. Two women got out, a redhead and a brunette—and if he hadn't been a married man, he would have said they weren't exactly hard on the eyes.

But it was their demeanor and carriage that alerted him to what Kendall was up to.

He looked at his wife.

"Fiona said I could bring some friends. So I brought nannies."

They walked like lions, smoothly and purposefully, gazing around them as they moved, their eyes alert. He knew at once what he was looking at. "I'd say those are bodyguards masquerading as nannies."

Kendall smiled. "I prefer to think of them as companions. And they're not available, so tell your brothers not to get any bright ideas. My nannies are not here for Callahan matchmaking."

Sloan grunted. Things were already tense on the ranch. Some of his brothers suffered more than others from itchy feet. Throwing hot, gorgeous, tough-minded females into the mix could only make a difficult situation hit the boiling point.

KENDALL SITUATED her babies and installed her "team" in their rooms. She hadn't been entirely honest with Sloan about the "nannies," but Fiona had heartily endorsed the plan. In fact, it had been Fiona's idea to bring "friends," to soothe Sloan's concerns about Kendall being at the ranch.

Fiona had called—to meddle, she said—and stressed her opinion, which was that it was important for a husband and a wife who had two new babies to spend time together as a family, if possible. Otherwise, mischief could set in. Families fell apart with too much time away from each other, especially when newlyweds didn't know one another very well. Kendall had taken Fiona's advice as a sage warning.

The extra protection gave Kendall a chance to return to Rancho Diablo. She wanted to look in on the bunkhouse project—but the thing she wanted above all was redemption. It wasn't easy knowing she'd given away crucial information to the enemy.

She had a lot to make up for.

It was the only way to keep her husband. And she intended to fight with everything she had for their marriage. For Isaiah and Carlos, she would do whatever she must to make sure their father understood just how much he meant in their little lives.

And in her own.

"THERE'S A LOT HAPPENING at Rancho Diablo," Fiona Callahan told her three friends as they sat at the Books'n'Bingo Society tearoom and bookshop with her. Here was the heartbeat of Diablo, New Mexico. Men might think they ran the show in town, but behind these flowery walls the social and civic decisions— plots, some said—were masterminded. "I fully expect fireworks."

Mavis Night, Corinne Abernathy and Nadine Waters gazed at her eagerly. "Tell us everything," Corinne said.

These were her best friends, her comrades-in-cahoots. From the first moment she'd arrived from Ireland to raise her nephews, these women had offered their friendship. In time, they'd taught her how Diablo worked, and they'd become her treasured sisters. "The mercenaries who hunted my sister and her husband are still plotting against us. They've sent a new group, which has caused no end of trouble, because this team is quite a bit more aggressive than the hired gun sent out before. They already kidnapped Kendall to get information out of her." Fiona sighed. "They didn't keep her long, but she's still living through the aftereffects of that."

"Oh, my," Nadine said. "Poor Kendall."

"So," Fiona said, "all my Callahans left. The chief

brought in Jeremiah's brother's family, who are fairly hardened, well-trained individuals in their own right."

"Gracious," Mavis said. "It sounds like all-out war."

Fiona nodded. "It is. Running Bear didn't want the babies on the ranch. No potential for hostages. The children and their families have responded wonderfully to their new lives. While they don't live under assumed identities or anything like that, they're surrounded all the time by staff, and their families, of course. The boys run ranch operations and Jonas's world-building projects quite easily from the Phillipses' compound and Dark Diablo. But," Fiona said, barely taking a breath, "Sloan and Kendall came to an impasse. He didn't want her here, because she'd been kidnapped, and that just about killed him. Of course, he can't be in Hell's Colony with her because his grandfather has got him here defending the ranch."

"My," Corinne said. "And those poor newborns need their parents to be together."

"Exactly." Fiona sighed. "That's the part that's killing me. Even when your nieces, Sabrina and Seton, had children by Sam and Jonas, we managed with pretty good success to keep them all in one place, despite great odds."

"For the most part." Mavis nodded. "So what are you planning?"

"Well," Fiona said, sipping her tea from a blue-willow cup, "I had Kendall bring friends with her from Hell's Colony. And when I say friends, I mean the kind that can kick ass and take names."

"Oh, happy day," Nadine said. "Sloan can't complain too much about Kendall being at Rancho Diablo, then."

"Exactly." Fiona's voice was triumphant. "And those two are just going to have to work out all their issues.

Hopefully, they'll realize how much they belong to-gether—with their babies."

"We'll do whatever we can to stir the pot," Corinne said, her blue eyes sparkling behind her polka-dotted glasses. "I mean help out, of course."

"Of course," Mavis said.

"Naturally," Nadine said. "We just love *helping*."

Fiona smiled. She had her own team right here—and they'd never let her down before.

Chapter Sixteen

A week later, Sloan wondered if it was his bride's plan to drive his brothers and particularly himself absolutely crazy.

"I can't take it," Dante said, peering out the window at the two nannies pushing the babies in big-wheeled prams.

"It's like catnip," his twin, Tighe, agreed. "Cowboy catnip."

"Don't look," Sloan said. "Sit by a wall with no windows. You're making me nuts." All their comments about the new nannies just made him realize how much he missed his wife. Since she'd been back at the ranch, Kendall hadn't shared her bed with him once. Hadn't invited him. Didn't even give him so much as a wink.

It was agony. He was having to live on the memories of those first few days in her bed.

His brothers' constant chatter about women was not helping.

"It's your test," Ash said, peering over their shoulders. "Hope you pass. Exams are notoriously difficult, you know. That's why they're called tests."

Galen sagged into a leather sofa. "I was the only one

good in school. All the rest of you were mental porcupines. Unmotivated, one might say."

"I had test anxiety, I'm pretty sure," Jace said, eyeballing the ladies. "Anyway, what teacher would give this test? It's cruel and unusual."

"Aunt Fiona," Ash said, blithely humored by her brothers' misery. "Kendall is a very willing accomplice, I'm betting."

Falcon looked at Sloan. "Is it possible that your wife has set some kind of temptation mousetrap for us?"

Sloan smiled. "I would never underestimate my wife."

Dante grunted. "You should defend her against specious claims."

Sloan noted his brothers gawking like teenagers, and shrugged. "Doesn't matter to me if she loads a mousetrap with the most delectable cheese she can find and then snaps your necks." He sighed. "You hammerheads were always destined either for marriage or misery, and I'm not sure they don't go together."

Ash giggled. "I think Kendall's smart as a whip. She told those beautiful bodyguards to take an evening stroll right at meeting time. Guaranteed to get your attention when you looked out the many windows of this fabulous library." Ash glanced at Sloan. "Makes me wonder what she's got up her sleeve for you."

"I don't know," he said, wishing Kendall did have something for him, and wishing it started with a kiss and ended with a satisfying "Oh, Sloan!" "Can we get on to the meeting, please? I think you've had enough time to drool on your bibs, bros."

Dante and Tighe tore themselves away from the windows.

"It's enough to sap a lesser man," Tighe said. "Fortunately, I can resist temptation."

"I can't," Dante said, "and I never try."

"Let's focus here," Sloan said. "We have ranch business to discuss."

"Why would it be us Fiona set the mousetrap for?" Galen, the one of them who liked to overuse his brain cells, said. "Why not you?" he asked Ash.

"Because I am not the weak link. Remember Grandfather said one of you is the weak link in the chain, the hunted one? The enemy knows this and will try to exploit it. But it's not me, so they don't have to worry about trying to matchmake me into staying here."

Sloan and his brothers stared at her.

"Well, don't look at me that way," Ash said. "It's true, if you would only use your skulls for something other than putting your hats on. It's not me. And Sloan, you're not totally safe, you know. Your marriage is not exactly built on anything more solid than one of Aunt Fiona's pies."

Didn't he know it. "This whole notion that my wife would plot with the capricious aunt worries me. Do petite, defenseless elderly women really plot?"

"Yes!" everyone in the room exclaimed.

Maybe they did. Sloan didn't know. "And why do we have a weak link again? Other than Tighe and Dante, who've never exactly been the most arrow-straight of the family, we're all pretty grounded."

His sister shrugged. "I didn't say it, the chief did. I never argue with Running Bear. It's pointless. He knows things none of us will ever know."

This was true. Sloan slumped back into the sofa. "I'm halfway to hell, I do believe."

"Better than being all the way," Falcon said cheerfully. "Now we just have to figure out how to survive the nine circles of hell and we'll all be good."

"As I see it," Ash said, "you lot are pretty much doomed. I easily envision a scenario in which I take over the entire twenty thousand acres of the new land. Which I intend to name Sister Diablo Ranch."

She received stunned looks from her brothers with delighted laughter. "Oh, yes. I will win. You're all too much of commitment phobes to be able to get it together. I'm not a commitment phobe. I'm happy to settle down."

"Tough luck for you," Jace said, "Sloan banished Xav to the outer edges of the ranch. He's doing canyon duty."

Ash leveled an ice-blue stare on Sloan. "Is that why Xav hasn't been around?"

Oh, boy. Here it came. Sloan shot Jace a dark look and shrugged. "Xav said he likes the canyons."

She blinked. "Oh."

The brothers fell silent. A man didn't want to be sent to the outer gates unless he wasn't emotionally invested in what was *inside* the gates. Sloan decided enough had been said tonight to give them all heartburn for weeks. "Can we get on with the meeting, or should we adjourn until we've all quit playing our tiny whiny fiddles? We have serious work to do around here that doesn't involve the opposite sex."

"I'm as opposite of sex as I've been in years," Dante said. "I agree with Sloan. Move to adjourn."

"I'm outta here," Ash said, and shot through the door.

"Did you have to do that?" Sloan demanded of Jace. "Did you have to roast her heart on a stick?"

"She doesn't need to look toward a man who can't make her happy," Jace pointed out.

"But she deserves the right to make up her own mind," Sloan said. He felt sorry for his sister, even if she did love torturing all of them just a bit with their own medicine.

"That little devil honestly thinks she's going to win all the land and give it a girlie name," Falcon said with a laugh. "And she probably will."

"Better get cracking, brothers," Galen said. "You may have just sent your sister out to set her own mousetrap. And I remind you that Ash has never, ever not done something she set her mind to."

"What about you?" Sloan demanded. "Don't you feel a need to have a kingdom of your own?"

"I don't," Galen said. "When this is all over, I believe I'll go get another specialty. I'm thinking about studying diseases and conditions of indigenous cultures."

"Always the books," Sloan muttered. "That's just hiding behind your big brain."

"Yeah, well, you'll be doing more reading than you've ever done in your life soon enough," Galen retorted. "Starting with *Goodnight Moon* and *Pat the Bunny.*"

"That's nice." Sloan went off irritated, not happy with anything at the moment. Out of sorts and bent out of shape.

Was he the weak link? The hunted one who could bring down the family?

It was a question that had begun to haunt him. Everyone else was doing their job, but he alone had his mind divided, torn in two directions.

He went off to find his wife.

SLOAN FOUND KENDALL IN the midst of moving baby paraphernalia and her own things into a truck. His sons were nowhere to be seen, but neither were the babelicious bodyguards—as some of his brothers referred to Kendall's "nannies"—so maybe that was a good thing. "What are you doing?"

"Moving to Sabrina and Jonas's house." Kendall looked up at him as she shoved some baby stuff carefully into the back of the truck. "Sabrina says they've been gone too many months, and that a house shouldn't sit still so long or things start going wrong. Since I have two nannies with me, and two babies, Jonas and Sabrina said we needed a place to stretch out. So they told me to move into their house."

Sloan was glad. For a moment, he'd been afraid she was leaving the ranch. Now that she was here, he was hoping for good things to happen. He didn't get to talk to Kendall often, but he did get to see his boys a lot, and that was enough to bring a smile to his face every day. "Could have mentioned it," he said, more roughly than he'd intended.

"I could have, but you'd have just found something to worry about, so I didn't." Kendall smiled at him and got in the truck. "I'm really looking forward to living in my own house. Even though it's not really mine, I won't feel like I'm roosting on top of everybody else now. I worry that the babies wake Fiona and Burke at night."

"They haven't mentioned it." Sloan shoved his hands in the pockets of his jeans. Even if Fiona heard the babies, she wouldn't mind. She'd just worry that maybe Kendall needed help.

He could help. How he wished that she was moving into a house they were sharing.

Then it occurred to him: he'd never asked her. Never thought about the two of them sharing a home. Well, he had thought about it, but he didn't have a house, and hadn't known when he would. So he felt stuck in between two worlds.

Kendall didn't feel stuck, obviously. She was moving on.

"We'll be only a few thousand yards away," she said, backing up the truck.

Sloan hopped in the passenger seat. "I'll help you unpack."

She smiled. "Thank you."

He wanted to offer her a home. But he didn't have one. He didn't know how long he would be here.

Unless he got the land across the canyons Aunt Fiona was dangling in front of them. "You ever think about us?"

Kendall glanced over at him as she drove. "I think about what's going to happen to us, and how it will affect the boys."

That wasn't exactly a ringing announcement that she envisioned him in her life. The two of them together. "Maybe we should have our own place."

She stopped the truck in front of Jonas's house. "Maybe." Going around to the back, she put the gate down and picked up a box.

He took it from her. "Maybe?"

She smiled up at him. "Maybe."

Was he looking for too much too soon? Sloan carried the box inside, amazed by the sight of his sons sleeping on a thick pallet on the floor, watched over by the nannies. The boys lay close together, wearing blue jean shorts and white T-shirts that read "Thing 1" and "Thing 2."

The sight stole Sloan's heart so fast he wasn't even aware it was gone. "Hey, little guys," he said, running a hand gently across their backs. He just wanted to feel them, their tiny, plump bodies so sweet and angelic they reminded him that there was still a lot of good in the world, and until this moment, maybe he hadn't remembered just how much.

The nannies melted away. Kendall knelt down next to him. "The outfits are your aunt Fiona's handiwork."

He smiled. "I'm not surprised."

"Your grandfather brought tiny moccasins." She showed him the small footwear, smiling.

"I didn't get them a gift. I didn't get *you* a gift." He looked at her. "Tell me what you want."

"When I think of something, I'll let you know."

He felt churlish. "Storm Cash brought the babies a gift. I think I left it in the barn."

"I know. Ash gave it to me. She said she knew I'd want to write a thank-you note."

There wasn't much to say to that. Sloan got up, glanced one last time at his sons, then at his beautiful wife. "I don't like Storm Cash."

"I know." Kendall nodded. "It's not a big deal. He brought a couple of baby blankets, which was sweet, but nothing that required anything more on my part than a formal acknowledgment."

Sloan felt a little better. "What about the nannies?"

"What about them?"

"I'm glad you have them." But he was uncomfortable, too, and decided that was because they spent time with Kendall that he couldn't. She didn't seem to be thawing all that much toward him. "Have you been out to see the bunkhouse?"

She shook her head. "I'm going this evening."

"I'll take you."

"Sloan, you don't have to. I have plenty of help."

"Yes, well, damn it, I'm your husband, and I'm tired of tiptoeing around that fact," he said, and her eyes went wide.

"Well, if you feel strongly about it, I'd love it if you went with me." Kendall smiled, and he felt as if he were melting under the sun. How was he ever going to explain to this woman that he might have married her because of the children, but that had been just an excuse for his real feelings?

KENDALL MADE SURE Ana and River were watching the babies—and that Sloan had taken off to do his watch duty—before she left her new abode. She got the military jeep and drove to the south end of the ranch, near the canyons. She checked her mobile, but there was no service.

She drove farther west, looking for any sign of her brother, and finally, she saw him, astride a horse, waving at her.

"What are you doing?" she demanded, when she drove near enough to yell at him. "I haven't seen you in days. I didn't know if you were dead or alive."

Her twin smiled at her ire. "I'm fine."

"That's not the point, Xav. You might not have been fine. Why are you hiding out down here? You look terrible." Her brother had changed so much from the man who used to help her run Gil Phillips, Inc., that she could barely believe it. His face wore several days' rough stubble, his jeans were dusty, his long-sleeved khaki shirt dirty. Even his brown Stetson was rimmed with a frosting of grit. "You have nephews at the house that would like to see you. And a shower would not be amiss."

His grin stretched wider. "It's good to see you, too, sis. Are you here just to give me heck?"

"Yes." She got out of the jeep, and he laughed. "What?"

"Where is my sister? What have you done with her?" He laughed so hard his horse stirred. "Where are your candy-colored stilettos and your business suit?"

She glared at him. "Haven't you heard I'm a mother now?" She glanced down at her cowboy boots, blue jean skirt and summery tank top. "Besides, it's comfortable. I was really worked up about getting my stiletto boots back, but that was just a pride thing." She admired the brown, basic Ropers she was wearing. "These are perfect."

He shook his head. "Amazing what Rancho Diablo does to a person."

"If Mom could see you, she'd faint." Kendall shrugged. "Oh, well. If you want to live like a dirty dog, that's your choice. But I think you're hiding out here for a reason."

"Maybe. Maybe not."

"It's dangerous," Kendall said, feeling a chill of something she couldn't name drift across her. "I don't like it here."

"You're not supposed to be away from the ranch house," Xav reminded her. "Sloan would be very tense if he knew you'd gone off where there's no cell service. How'd you know where to find me?"

"Lucky guess."

"If I hadn't spotted you, you'd never have found me. Don't come down here by yourself, Kendall. It really isn't safe for a woman."

"I've already been dragged off by Sloan's stupid uncle. What's the worst that could happen to me now?"

"I don't know. But worse."

"I'm safer than anybody at Rancho Diablo. You have no idea how safe I am."

"How is everybody at the ranch?" he asked, and Kendall knew exactly who he was asking about, because he was her twin, and she recognized the sound of longing in his voice.

"You're an idiot," she said. "I know what you're doing."

"You might, but I don't. It just feels right, and I accept that."

She sniffed. "If you want to know about certain people, you'll have to come back to find out. I'm living in Jonas and Sabrina's house now, so look for me and the boys there."

"Wait," Xav said, following her as she got into the jeep. "Throw me a bone here."

"No." She started the jeep. "It's not a bone you need. It's a haircut and a woman."

"You know, sis," he said, propping one boot up on the jeep's running board, "you're not exactly in better shape than me. Word on the street is that your marriage may not be of the lasting variety."

She looked at Xav. "How would you know? You haven't been near a street in weeks." She pushed his boot off the jeep runner and drove away with a wave.

She was working on her marriage the only way she knew how, by being right here on Rancho Diablo. Whatever it took, she was going to win back her place in the Callahan clan.

And she just might have been on that path, except for the tall man suddenly standing in her way. Wolf.

She could drive around him, but if he wanted to talk, he'd make that happen eventually, anyway.

Besides, she'd never been one to back down from a fight.

Chapter Seventeen

"Let me guess," Kendall said. "You're here to return my boots."

Wolf grinned. "No. But I will say that you're a tough cookie, almost tough enough for me to admire."

She glanced around. "Where are your goons?"

"They sent their regrets. They said they'd miss getting to chat with you."

Kendall grimaced in annoyance. "Look. Just cut to the chase. I know that you're the bad uncle, the black sheep of the family. You're trying to make trouble, and so you're hanging around. What do you want from me?"

"Maybe I like talking to you."

She gazed at his scarred face and big frame. "Whatever information you seek, I don't have it, Mr. Callahan."

"Chacon. We're all Chacon, even Jeremiah. He took his wife's family name to elude the cartel that wanted to talk to him. Let me ride shotgun," Wolf said, getting into the passenger seat. "I'll show you something."

"We've already spent far too much time together, Mr. Chacon. Get out."

He sighed. "I mean you no harm. If I had, I would have already made it happen."

"You do mean me harm, because you're after the Callahans, who are my family. I don't care what you want with me. I've had twins since our last meeting. I'm too busy to care about your family tree. Do you have children, Wolf? Well, it doesn't matter," she said, going on without waiting for an answer. "Once you've had kids, all the world may be a stage, but all a mother can think about are her own little actors. And now, if you don't mind, I must end this meeting. It's about time for my sons' dinner, and they don't like to wait."

Wolf got out of the jeep. "We'll chat again."

"I hope not. I have nothing you need, and you know that. Quite frankly, you're wasting your time."

"Then I'll try someone else in the future."

Chills of foreboding teased Kendall. "I don't know how anybody can help you if no one has the information you're seeking."

"You'd be surprised what people will share when they're…convinced."

"Now you're threatening me. And I don't like to be threatened," Kendall said with some heat. "Look, you can hang around the ranch all you want, but I'm pretty certain you'll die here and get picked apart by the vultures."

"I'll find Jeremiah and Molly, and Julia and Carlos, eventually," he said, his voice soft.

"You'd sell out your own brothers?" Kendall asked in disbelief. "Where I come from, family is everything."

"I know. You know, Ms. Phillips, after you so kindly shared all that information about your family, I had it looked into. I have to give you credit for finding a place to hide the Callahans where they are almost safe. Everything has gated access, and there are private guards. I even detected a sniper on the roof," he said, his tone deceptively admiring. "Which at first astonished me, but then I remembered that your corporation is international, and you'd be familiar with travel that involves armed guards. Even if one takes a simple trip to the more scenic and remote areas of South America or Africa, there are armed guards. And then I realized that you're a formidable ally."

"Your point?" Kendall said, beginning to think her best option might be to lay a few jeep tracks on this odious man. Secretly, she was horrified that he'd been so close to Jonas and the rest of the clan. But he wouldn't have told her if he meant harm there—at least she hoped.

"This is a large ranch, with a few working oil wells and so much silver the wealth can be quantified as immense. The land value alone is astounding, not to mention the fine houses. And you're doing such a good job on the new bunkhouse. Who would have ever imagined a bunkhouse needed a bilevel library?"

She shook her head. "You're disgusting. You want to kill your brothers so you can take over Rancho Diablo? It's in Callahan hands."

"All that can be changed. This land was bought by the tribe. My father, Running Bear, turned this portion over to Jeremiah, who left it in his wife's sister's control. And don't let us forget the mystical Diablos, spiritual wealth that is more important than gold. Still all under Fiona's control." He smiled. "Dotty old woman to be running such a large empire, I think."

Kendall got his meaning. It was too hard to get to the Callahans, because the Phillipses' compound was secure. Wolf's reasoning was that Fiona would make a far better hostage. Kendall's skin crawled. "You make me sick."

"You could find out what I want to know. Where my brothers are hiding means nothing to you."

"I thought they were all dead," Kendall said, buying time. "Jonas believes his parents are deceased." It wasn't true, of course. But she didn't have to admit that she knew anything. "And Sloan never mentioned his parents to me."

"I figure you're more valuable to me as an informant," Wolf said. "I could take you as a hostage, but I think you can find out what I want to know without things having to get dirty."

"If Jeremiah and Molly and Julia and Carlos were alive, how would anyone know where they were?" Kendall wasn't sure on this point. Jonas had never taken her into his confidence about it, and Sloan barely talked to her about his parents. They didn't talk much about personal things.

They didn't talk much at all, which wasn't good in a marriage. Even if she'd nearly destroyed their relationship by giving away family secrets, she loved Sloan. She wouldn't hurt him.

"I assume your sons mean a lot to you," Wolf said, lighting a small, thin cigar. "I bet you're a good mother. I noticed that you hired two military-trained operatives to push their sweet little carriages." He smiled. "It's a touching sight, one that people don't usually get to see—military operatives pretending to be nannies.

"You almost fooled me, Ms. Phillips. At first I was surprised that you had access to such well-trained help. But then I remembered the sniper at Hell's Colony, and I did some checking. You had two brothers in the military. With your family's fortune, you can afford the best so-called *nannies* available. But good help is harder to find than one knows."

Wolf's smile was ghastly, hideous and foul. "I need that information, and I need it soon. I believe your sons have a three-month birthday coming up, don't they?"

Kendall drove off, her blood ice in her veins. She was a pawn. Sloan had to know what Wolf had in mind.

On the other hand, maybe his uncle was bluffing.

She couldn't underestimate him. He'd threatened Fiona and her boys. She was going to have to tell Sloan.

He'd be mad as hell that she'd gone to the canyons.

Kendall didn't have very long to consider her options, because Sloan met her as she pulled in, his eyes blazing as he sat astride a black gelding.

"I've got to go feed the babies," she said, parking the jeep and heading in to her new abode.

The nannies looked up, smiling, but Ash shook her head at Kendall. "Fair warning, brother's got a bee in his Stetson," she said.

"Ana, River, do you mind feeding the boys? I'm going to my room," Kendall said, and went up to take a bath. Anything to not face her husband until she'd gathered her thoughts. Calmed down. Tried to figure out Wolf's ultimate plan and why he was determined to use her in his terrible scheme.

The bedroom door flew open. Kendall whirled around.

"Do you mind?" she demanded of Sloan.

"I do mind," he said. "I mind having the mother of my children running around in places where it's not even safe for armed men." He crossed the floor and tipped her chin up so she had to look at him. "I've always admired your independence, but your independence isn't your best asset here."

"Your uncle isn't after me. He's after you."

"And he'll use you to get to me. Which will destroy me, Kendall. Our sons deserve to have their mother with them."

"Wolf's not going to hurt me. He knows I'm useless except as a messenger."

"What's the message?" Sloan's eyes were hooded.

"That he wants Rancho Diablo." She reached out to draw Sloan into her arms, then held him tight, worried more about her marriage than his uncle and his plans. "I, too, have a message for you, Sloan."

"Which is what?" He waited, his gaze watchful.

"I want you in my bed," Kendall said. "Make love to me. I'm so very scared I'm going to lose you forever."

His eyes flared. He didn't move a muscle. It was as if he was frozen, unsure.

She was sure. And she was going to fight for her marriage. No matter what the mercenary in the canyons thought, she could beat him. Wolf's plan to drive them apart couldn't work, because she loved her husband more than she'd ever dreamed she could love a man.

If there was war on the ranch, then she intended to use all her weapons. She pulled off her boots, took off her summery tank top, slid off her blue jean skirt.

And that was all it took to get her husband back in her arms at last.

Tighe and Dante stared at the two bodyguards as they rode around the indoor corral, amazed at the sight of the two women riding. "I didn't know they did anything besides protect Kendall and our nephews," Tighe said.

"Look at the seats on those fine ladies," Dante said, his voice full of longing. "Too cute for words."

Jace came up behind them. "You beat me to it."

"To what?" Tighe asked, barely glancing at his brother. The three of them stayed concealed behind a low wall, letting their eyes take in the poetry in motion in front of them.

"I was going to see if I could give them a lesson or two in staying in the saddle," Jace said. "Looks like this isn't their first time."

The three men stared, watching the bounce and sway of female body parts as they went around the ring in the indoor arena. Tighe thought morosely that three was a crowd. There were enough women for him and one other brother, and one brother was going to be disappointed. He kind of had his eye on the little redhead. He'd never had a redhead before, and that one seemed a bit sparky. But the brunette was real easy on the eyes, too.

"How'd you know they'd be riding?" Tighe asked.

"Kendall gave them the night off." His brother's head was like an oscillating fan as he watched them go around.

"Is Ash watching Kendall and the babies?" Dante asked.

"Apparently, she's been sent to keep an eye on Fiona and Burke. Sloan is with Kendall," Jace said, and they all went, "Oh."

"Family time," Tighe said. "The four of them, finally."

"I didn't think Sloan was going to be able to resist Kendall forever," Jace said. "Just like I'm not going to be able to resist those two."

"Two?" Tighe glared at his brother. "There's a short-age of women around here, dunce. You don't get two."

"I can have two," Jace said. "I'm the only one in the family who really wants to settle down. Even Sloan doesn't really want to settle down. He's still wild in the head. Not me. I *know* the value of a good woman. I figure I'll go out with both those bodyguards, and let them raffle me off. And then I'll get the land. I'm going to name it Navajo Wind Ranch. Haven't decided if I want to raise cattle or veggies. Or both." Jace sighed with contentment as he finished his soliloquy.

Tighe shook his head. "You're an idiot. You're not going to get the ranch."

"Got more of a chance than either of you do," Jace retorted, but then they both realized that Dante wasn't there anymore. Tighe's twin had saddled a horse and joined the ladies, determined to figure out a way to grab some female company for himself.

"Look at him go," Jace murmured. "What a show-boat."

Dante *was* a showboat, Tighe thought, watching his brother do tricks on the back of his gelding. Though they could all ride like the wind, had been born in the saddle, Dante was the master of tricks. And he was certainly showing everything he had, practically turn-ing himself into a pretzel weaving over and under his horse as it cantered. At one point he even stood on his hands on the saddle.

"Dang," Jace said, "what a show-off."

Yeah, but Show-off had gotten the girls to stop and admire him. Tighe realized he was about to be out-gunned, and that would leave only one lady on the loose. He had his eye on the one with the dark cherry hair, so he went to the barn office, while Jace was still complaining about some brothers being attention hogs.

Grabbing a large rubber band, Tighe fitted an impressive "wasp" to it, a tightly twisted wad of paper that would sting nicely on impact. Casually, he stood in the shadows, and the next time Dante's horse cantered around, his showboating twin balanced perfectly on his hands on the back of his mount, Tighe took aim at his brother's wrist.

Fired hard.

Dante went flipping off his horse, with a satisfying yowl when he hit the ground. Whistling, Tighe went to mount his own horse, to do a little strutting of his own.

THE RANCH WAS QUIET. It was a dark, hot evening; much of New Mexico was suffering. There was talk of fires burning in parts of the state. Ash felt so fortunate that fire hadn't started here.

But nights like this were long and torturous when she didn't have to work. Kendall and Sloan had given her the night off so they could have alone time together with their boys. Ash hoped her brother was smart enough to work things out with his bride. She wouldn't put money on it, but sometimes Sloan surprised her.

Since she didn't have to guard Kendall or the boys, she went to check on Fiona and Burke. They, too, shooed her off, telling her that they were boarded up in their bedroom for some Saturday night romance. Which had made her laugh at first, until she realized Fiona was probably just plucky enough to still run Burke around the bedroom plenty.

"Sheesh," Ash said. "Now what do I do with myself?"

She knew exactly what she *wanted* to do. She wanted to go to the canyons and find Xav, ask him why the heck he was avoiding her. Okay, she wouldn't be that obvious about it, but she definitely wanted to find him and give him something to think about. She had eyes for that cowboy, and she had a funny feeling Xav knew it.

And had run away.

"Big chicken," she said, and headed to the canyons.

"Is ASHLYN GONE?" Fiona asked Burke, as her husband peered out the window of their bedroom.

"Yes. I just heard the door slam. And she's walking across to the barn. Probably intends to do a little riding."

"It's not easy to get to plan shenanigans with all these people watching me," Fiona complained. "Remember the good old days, when it was just me and you, pulling everyone's strings like puppeteers?" She sighed, feeling very put upon. "Between Running Bear and Kendall, this place is guarded tighter than a jail."

"Let's get while the getting's good." Burke led her down the stairs. "You never know when someone will come to check on us. This whole family thinks we're in need of constant monitoring."

"We shouldn't complain. I try to think of it as getting our just deserts for all the years we monitored the boys like protective hens." She followed her husband outside into the darkness, hopped into the passenger seat of the van. "We have to be quick. I don't know how long I bought Ashlyn off with our romantic interlude story."

"Could be a few hours. They won't check again until dinner."

"They won't look for a meal tonight." Fiona put the

basket she'd carried out with her at her feet. "I have no idea what Storm Cash's modus operandi is, but since he's stopped in on us a couple of times, I say it's time we return the hospitality. My blackberry pie ought to smooth the way."

Chapter Eighteen

When Sloan awakened the next morning at his custom-ary four-thirty to start ranch chores, he was amazed to find Kendall gone. Which was a shame, because he was really hoping to find her beside him. He loved the smell of her hair and the feel of her skin, and they hadn't had enough of a marriage yet for him to really explore those wonderful sensations she gave him.

He walked into the den, smiling as he saw her asleep on the sofa, the babies on a soft, fluffy pallet next to her. His sons must have needed a feeding, and like a cad, he'd slept through the event. He looked at the three beautiful people who'd changed his life, and felt his heart lift inside him.

Little Carlos opened his eyes, looking right at him. Sloan could see his son watching him, knew he was absolutely aware that someone was nearby. He would have sworn he saw trust in the baby boy's eyes. "Hi," he said, squatting down next to him. He put his fin-ger into his hand, and Carlos clenched it. Though he knew it was impossible, Sloan would have sworn his son wanted to be picked up and held.

So he did, cradling him against his chest. His brother slept on, undisturbed, as did their mother.

"Let's go have some coffee," he told Carlos, and carried him into the kitchen with him. "It's important not to wake Mom when she's getting a little rest."

Carlos didn't move, didn't protest, as Sloan started the coffee and got out a couple of mugs. There was some fruit on the counter, so he grabbed a bit of that and a muffin. He put Carlos in his carrier and set him on the counter where he could watch. He seemed interested in what his father was doing, and suddenly it occurred to Sloan that his son looked an awful lot like his namesake, Sloan's own father.

It had been years since he'd seen his parents, but he remembered when they'd left, and had realized that everything had changed. Learned that danger could come no matter how good you were, and that his parents had been freedom fighters of a sort. They'd infiltrated and spied on the cartel that wanted free rein of this ranch land, running drugs and contraband over it.

"You'd be proud of your grandparents," he told Carlos. "Through your veins runs the blood of a man who fought for what he loved."

Carlos looked at him, his round face and jewel-bright eyes focused on Sloan. "You're listening to everything I say, aren't you?"

Suddenly a smile bloomed on the baby's face. Sloan chuckled. "Okay, now you're just sucking up to dear old dad. I have a funny feeling you're the one who'll be the daredevil…oh, brother," he said, picking up his son and holding him so he could look down into his eyes. "I forgot you also have Aunt Fiona's genes. You're a triple whammy. No one will stand a chance against you and your brother."

Sloan took his coffee cup and his son and went outside, content. Prouder than he'd ever been in his life.

"Hello, little man," Falcon said, walking by. "Nice of you to get your ugly daddy up this morning. But both of you are late. I had to start your chores."

"That's fine," Sloan said, suddenly obsessed by a desire to go back and be with the rest of his family, who were no doubt still snoozing away. "I'll let you do them today."

Falcon laughed. "Going back to bed?"

"If I'm lucky," Sloan said, and carried his son back inside the house.

Isaiah and Kendall slept on, completely undisturbed by his moving around in the kitchen. He changed Carlos's diaper and put him back on the pallet next to his brother, and then carried his wife to her bed so she could rest. She stirred, but not much, and when he covered her with a sheet, she curled right into her pillow.

He wouldn't mind joining her. But right now he had sons who wanted to read the morning paper with him. And they were about to do just that when Sloan's phone buzzed with a text from Ash.

Have you seen aunt and uncle?

His blood ran cold as ice water.

"What are you doing?" Kendall asked, coming out of the bedroom.

"I was going to read the paper to the boys," Sloan said, "but Ash can't find Aunt Fiona and Burke."

"That's odd. Ash sticks to them like glue."

He nodded. "I'm sorry. I hate to be a deserter, but I feel like I need to go lay eyes on them."

Kendall smiled. "It's all right. Be sure and check the basement. You know how Fiona likes to putter with her holiday decorations and canned goods down there."

Sloan wanted to tell Kendall how much he enjoyed being with her, how much last night had meant to him. But this wasn't really the time. She looked ruffled and darling in a blue nightgown and her blond hair just a bit tousled.

He wished he had time to tousle it a bit more.

That thought would have to wait.

"WHY DID YOU LEAVE THEM?" Sloan asked Ash, as he and his brothers gathered up in the darkness of the early morning.

His little sister looked miserable. "They said they wanted some alone time."

"Alone time?" Jace said. "What exactly does that mean? They're always alone."

"They're never alone," Ash said. "I'm always in the house with them."

"Why is that a problem?" Tighe demanded. "You don't take up much space. The house is huge. It's a mansion."

"I think they wanted some *alone* time," Ash repeated, and suddenly, Sloan got it.

"Oh. Alone time." He scratched under his hat. "Well, you should have stood post outside."

"Don't be weird," Ash said. "They didn't want anybody around. You won't want to admit this, Sloan, but Fiona's still got a bit of a gleam in her eye for her husband. There's a strong possibility she might use whipped cream for more than putting on your peach pie. And when she said, 'Go,' I said, 'Yes, ma'am.'"

His brothers laughed, slapped him on the back. As if he was the only one who was worried out of his gourd.

"They probably went into town. Their van is gone," Sloan said.

"At this hour?" Galen shook his head. "What would be open?"

"She could have gone to the Books'n'Bingo," Dante suggested. "That's her home away from home, and they do own it."

Sloan blinked. "They do?"

"Yeah. She runs it with her three friends, but Fiona's name is on the paperwork." Jace shrugged. "I saw it when I was going through some computer files. And speaking of computer files, did you know Fiona keeps a ranch journal?"

The brothers all stared at him. "Please don't tell me you've been reading her personal papers," Sloan said.

"No, it's a *ranch* journal," Jace emphasized. "Like a daily accounting of events."

"Aka, a private diary," Sloan said crossly.

"No. This doesn't begin with 'Dear Diary.'" Jace glared at him. "I think I know the difference between a register and a journal! This is more of a business document!"

"All right, grab your hat out of orbit and put it back on your silly head," Sloan said. "Why are you telling us about it?"

"Because," Jace said, having the grace to look a bit shamefaced, "you might be interested to know that ten years ago, Fiona sold a bunch of horses to Storm Cash."

"He wasn't living here ten years ago," Sloan said. "He's a new neighbor."

"Very coincidental, too, I thought," Jace said. "Apparently, the deal was such a good one that at one point they discussed doing business together again. Maybe even going into business together. But for some reason, Fiona changed her mind. They definitely know each other, though. He's not the stranger we thought him to be."

Which made Sloan wonder exactly who'd thrown that rock through the library window that night if it hadn't been Storm Cash. Wolf? He didn't think so. Small stuff wasn't his style. He'd go for a kidnapping and some coercion, as he had with Kendall.

"I'm going to talk to Storm," Sloan said. "The rest of you stay on post."

"I'm coming," Ash said. "I lost them, I'm going to find them."

"Where were you, exactly, when you lost our aunt and uncle, Ash?" Dante asked, and when his sister blushed, Sloan groaned.

"When I get back, we're going to hash this out," he said. "The mission hasn't changed. And everyone needs to remember that mistakes happen if we let down our guard. That's exactly when something will go wrong."

He headed to his truck, Ash on his heels.

Kendall stood at the passenger-side door, the babies in her arms. "I'm going," she said. "Ash, you watch the boys. The bodyguards will be back on duty in an hour. You can call them now if you want to, because they'll come. But if Sloan's going to find Fiona and Burke, I'm going with my husband."

Ash looked at Sloan. He nodded, and she took the babies from Kendall.

"I shouldn't let you," Sloan said, and Kendall said, "Try and stop me."

He grinned, and opened the truck door for his opinionated wife.

"I DON'T WANT YOU treating me like a delicate flower just because I've had your children," Kendall told Sloan as he started the truck and headed down the drive. "It's not necessary."

"How do you expect me not to?" he asked, driving a few miles per hour more than allowed toward Storm's ranch. "Every man wants to protect his wife and the mother of his children."

"We're a team," Kendall insisted. "Anyway, I messed things up. I want to be part of the solution."

"Kendall, Wolf would have figured out where our cousins were eventually. We just tried to buy time by getting the family out to Dark Diablo and Hell's Colony, where they could settle in and get security details outfitted. Wolf doesn't even know some of the Callahans are at Dark Diablo. He thinks everyone is at the impenetrable fortress you call home."

"I call home wherever you are," Kendall said. "You're just going to have to get used to that."

He couldn't help smiling. "I'm getting used to it."

"Good." She adjusted her seat belt, peered outside to see if she could spot Fiona's van returning. They barely saw any vehicles, none Callahan. "They're not going to appreciate us micromanaging them. Your aunt and uncle are very independent."

"They can't just disappear— Look," he said, pulling off the road.

The family van Fiona always drove was on the shoulder, with no hazard lights blinking. Kendall jumped out of the truck and ran over, jerking open the door to peer inside. "They're not here."

Sloan glanced around. "I'm calling Falcon. Let him know we may need backup on horseback. Look for footprints. Anything that might tell us which way they went."

Kendall looked in every direction. "There was a

struggle," she said softly, her skin crawling with fear, "unless Fiona was unusually clumsy and dropped her treasured blackberry pie." She pointed to the smashed pie spilling from its once-beautiful crust.

Sloan looked at her. "I want you to take my truck and go back home. Get Ash. Tell her I need her on horseback. Some of our best mounts, ones that aren't afraid of dark caves."

"Do you want me to call Sheriff Cartwright?" Kendall climbed into the truck.

"Not yet. I don't want the tracks obscured. It may be our only hope of locating them."

Kendall drove off, hurrying to Rancho Diablo. She parked Sloan's truck and flew into the house.

To her shock, Ash was gone. The babies were gone.

"Ashlyn!" Kendall shrieked. Grabbing her gun and stuffing it in her purse, she hurried to the main house, her heart pounding. Maybe Ash had brought the babies there for security reasons.

She prayed harder than she'd ever prayed before.

A soft, deep voice made her start as she walked into the kitchen, and Kendall slowed, listening. She definitely heard Fiona. It sounded as if they were going down into the basement. She moved quietly toward the stairs.

"Open up the safe, old woman," she heard a man say, and Kendall froze. There was no safe downstairs, just canned fruits and vegetables Fiona had put by so she could bake and cook healthy food all winter.

Kendall pulled out her phone, texted her husband. Here. In the basement.

She hit Send, right before someone grabbed her.

Kendall swung her bag, completely forgetting about the heavy gun in her purse. She caught her assailant across the temple, amazed that he let go and went down like a sack of bricks. In the darkness she couldn't see who it was, but she wasn't hanging around to find out, either. He'd come to soon enough.

She headed down the stairs, gun drawn.

Fiona and Burke stood under the old fluorescent light, looking annoyed. Kendall wasn't surprised that they weren't exactly cowering in their shoes; they were stronger than most people.

She saw a boot just past the doorway. It was black and dusty.... She'd seen that boot before.

Wolf.

"Open it up, Fiona. We're burning daylight, and I plan to be far away from here really soon."

Fiona barely glanced at Kendall, telegraphing that she saw her but was being careful not to give that fact away.

"There's no safe down here," Fiona said. "I don't know why you think that, Wolf."

"I know you have the Navajo silver here. I know Running Bear hid it at Rancho Diablo. And you're his partner." Wolf laughed. "It took me a few years to figure out that my father had hidden it right under my nose, and this basement is the perfect place to hide a large amount of silver. It came to me when I saw the basement being dug at the new bunkhouse."

"You should be ashamed," Fiona said. "Aren't you ashamed of yourself? There is no upside to being the family black sheep."

"Open the safe before I shoot your husband," Wolf said, at which point Kendall took careful aim at the black boot, praying her hands stayed steady and that she'd learned her shooting lessons from Falcon well.

A howl rent the air. The boot disappeared from sight

as hell broke out. Wolf ran up the stairs, pushing her against the wall as he passed. Kendall ran forward and hugged Fiona and Burke.

Suddenly, she heard boots thundering down the stairs. Sloan appeared in the basement, his gaze sweeping her.

"We're fine," Kendall said. "Go!"

He ran off, and Kendall finally released Fiona and Burke. "You gave us such a scare!"

"I gave myself a scare," Fiona said. "Goodness, what a nasty man."

"Whatever were you thinking, sneaking off like that?" Kendall demanded. Relief flooded her, making her ask the very question she figured was the worst to ask at this moment.

Fiona sighed. "I'll tell you later. Let's go upstairs and get Burke a toddy. I think he needs one."

Kendall followed Fiona, turning off the light and closing the door to the basement behind them. Sloan stood over someone who lay in a heap on the floor.

She flipped on a light. "Who is it?"

"A woman." Sloan looked at her. "Who hit her?"

"I did," Kendall said. She stepped close to look at the woman on the ground, who was still out cold. "I know her. She's one of Wolf's gang."

"A merc."

Falcon burst in the door, halting as he saw the unconscious woman. "Oh, man, we don't hit women, Sloan."

"I know that!" Sloan glared at his brother. "Kendall gave her a small headache. She'll be fine in a few."

Falcon looked at Kendall. "You're coming along nicely."

"Sloan," Kendall said, "I can't find Ashlyn. I can't find the babies."

"We're up here," Ash said, her voice floating down from upstairs. "I brought the twins here once the text went around that Fiona and Burke were missing. Figured being in the main house was safest because of the attic." She came down the staircase, wearing two carriers, one in front of her, one in back, papoose-style. "I didn't mean to scare anyone. But it never hurts to be cautious. And Sheriff Cartwright is on the way. Our brothers are tracking Wolf."

Kendall nearly fainted with relief. "Oh, thank God!" She ran to kiss her babies.

"They're fine. Getting hungry, I think." Ash glanced at Sloan. "I didn't realize Wolf had Fiona and Burke until I heard his voice in the stairwell. By then, Kendall was already on top of things. You should have heard her take out that guard." She smiled at her sister-in-law. "I had your back, but it seemed clear you had the situation in hand. The babies and I thought it was best to lie low. They, of course, never woke up. They're not interested in drama."

Kendall smiled, feeling at last like she belonged. It mattered so much to her to be part of the fight for the ranch and the people she loved.

Expressionless, Sloan reached to take one of his sons' carriers from Ash. "You guys wrap this up. I'm taking my wife and boys home. Our family has a lot to discuss."

Kendall took Isaiah from Ash and followed Sloan. They definitely had a lot to talk about—but then again, talking could be overrated when there were other things she wanted to do with her outlaw man.

"This can't go on," Sloan told his wife. "I don't want you taking on trained killers, Kendall."

She set the babies in the playpen, bristling. "What do you suggest I should have done differently?"

"Let us handle it. That's what we're here for."

"I wasn't going to let anything happen to Fiona and Burke, and at that moment, I was the only one around." Kendall glared at Sloan. "While I appreciate your concerns, I feel that they're unfounded. I would never jeopardize myself or my family."

"But you did," he said, not certain how he was going to get her to understand that she was a mother, not a warrior. "When you came back here, you assured me that your bodyguards would be doing the defending. You said you wouldn't be in a position again to be taken hostage." He couldn't really explain to his wife how badly she'd worried him. Their children needed her. *He* needed her. "But that's not the way it's worked out."

She put her hands on her hips. He prepared himself for gale-force blowback. "Sloan, you're my husband. Not my keeper. You need to deal with that, and we'll both be a lot happier."

He tipped her chin so he could look her into her eyes. "Kendall, you mean the world to me. You're a special woman. But I don't want you fighting. This isn't your battle."

"It's a family fight," Kendall said. "I'm part of this family. You made me part of the things that matter to Rancho Diablo and the Callahans." She moved away, and he dropped his hand. "I don't understand what you wanted me to do. Walk off? Cower in the hall and let Wolf hurt your aunt and uncle?" She shook her head. "Sloan, I've never been the kind of woman to look around for a man to solve my problems. It perplexes me that you expect it of me. Fiona isn't the kind of lady who waits for people to take care of her, and your sister is certainly no shrinking violet. I'm guessing your mother wasn't exactly a retiring, timid individual if she was in the CIA and is now in witness protection. There are no dependent do-nothings in your family tree. Why would you expect it of me?"

He glanced over at his sons. Small and soft now, they'd grow up as fierce as anyone in their bloodline, he figured. "Because I need it this way right now," Sloan said with a sigh. "We can handle our own battles."

She stared at him for the longest time. Sloan could tell she was measuring her thoughts and emotions against his words. Finally, she said, "I'm sorry. That's just not who I am. And I can't change, any more than you can."

She was his whole heart, his world, along with these boys. Sloan knew Kendall wanted to be at his side in all things, Callahan in everything. But he didn't want his wife kidnapped or embroiled in a confrontation. There were enough warriors around to defend Rancho Diablo.

The worst part was that Kendall was right. Though Ash had been upstairs, she wouldn't have abandoned the babies to rescue Fiona and Burke. Ash had called Sheriff Cartwright, but he and his deputies and officers wouldn't have been here in time.

Sloan knew Kendall had done the right thing—but that didn't mean he liked it. Or that he could live with it.

KENDALL WAS SO DISGUSTED with her husband that she took the babies into town for a ride in the double stroller the next day. She didn't want to be around his stubborn, ornery self. Claiming she needed the rest, he'd slept on the sofa, the babies on the pallet next to him.

He obviously wasn't coming to her bed, and frankly, she'd been too steamed to care. Which wasn't the way she wanted her marriage.

"Look," she told the babies, "a bookstore. Let's go find you a book." She looked up at the sturdy pink awning over the Books'n'Bingo Society, deciding this was just what she needed: a glass of tea, a cookie and a book.

She pushed the stroller inside, where she was greeted by a woman with polka-dotted glasses and a cheery smile.

"Hello," she said. "I'm Corinne Abernathy. I know who you are. You're Kendall Phillips from Hell's Colony who married Sloan Chacon Callahan. And these are your boys." She beamed. "The three of us ladies—Nadine, Mavis and I—sent over baby gifts. And we received your sweet thank-you note." She beamed, delighted when she spied two other ladies. "Mavis! Nadine! Come see the newest residents of Diablo!"

Her friends hurried over. Corinne showed Kendall to a chair, and the ladies picked up the babies, thrilled to take them around the small tearoom to show off to the other customers.

"What can I get you, dear?" Corinne asked.

Kendall hadn't even looked at a menu. "I came in here for a glass of tea, a cookie and a book."

Corinne smiled. "What period?"

"Excuse me?"

"The book, dear. What genre and period, approximately? I'll see what we have that's close."

"Um…" Kendall couldn't think. "Something romantic. Relaxing."

"All right. So peach tea, a few cookies and perhaps the history of Diablo. Written by some of the locals."

Corinne beamed. "There's quite a bit of romance, as you might imagine. And since you're a permanent resident here now, you want to catch up on the history, I'm sure."

Kendall nodded. "I'd love to read that. But I'm not sure I'm exactly a permanent resident."

"Oh, Diablo gets in one's blood, dear. I'll go get your order."

She went into the kitchen, placing an assortment of delicate cookies on a flower-patterned china plate. She poured a glass of tea, and as Mavis and Nadine rushed in with the babies to get the scoop on Kendall, Corinne sighed. "She's not sure she's a permanent resident. I'd say it's time for us to do a little encouraging."

They trotted back out, their mission in mind.

"Here's your tea and an assortment of sweets." Corinne set everything down. "I'll get your copy of *Love, Diablo Style* out to you in a moment. You'll enjoy it, I'm sure. Our local writers really know how to tell a yarn."

Kendall smiled. "Thank you."

Nadine took Isaiah in her lap. "These babies are growing so much that I can hardly believe it."

"I know." Kendall looked at her boys. "I can't, either."

"Before you know it, they'll be riding," Mavis said. "And then it'll be time to enroll them in school. And then send them off to college. It all happens so fast, doesn't it, Corinne?"

Corinne nodded. "Indeed. But we're so happy to have you here in Diablo where we can watch these little angels grow up."

Kendall looked at each of the women, studying them. "Thank you for your kindness."

"You feel free to come to us anytime you need anything," Nadine said. "We love to babysit. And as you probably know, Sabrina and Seton, who married Jonas and Sam Callahan, are Corinne's nieces. Corinne knows a little something about Callahan men."

Kendall smiled. "I've met your nieces many times. They're wonderful women."

"And so are you," Corinne said, applying the soothing balm liberally. "I won't say that Callahan men aren't a handful, but the ladies who catch them seem very happy."

The three women looked at Kendall, their eyes large and encouraging.

And Kendall didn't know why she said it—she wasn't the type to engage in personal chitchat—but she heard herself confiding, "My husband and I disagree on my role at the ranch. I see myself as a partner, sharing everything, the good times and the bad."

"And Sloan?" Nadine asked, and the three women leaned forward to hear every word.

"Sloan seems to want a spouse who is willing to stay in the background and be a wife and mother." Kendall thought about it, making sure her statement was fair. "He's a good man, a wonderful father."

"But so Callahan," Nadine said, and Kendall smiled.

"That's a plus most of the time," she said.

"They can be ornery." Corinne's eyes twinkled. "Believe me, we all know. This town runs on ornery. We're not afraid of ornery. What we worry about is uncommitted."

"Oh," Kendall said, "I think Sloan's definitely committed." He'd never indicated to her that he didn't want to be married, just the opposite.

"Wasn't Sloan the loner?" Mavis asked. "I think

Fiona said that of all of them, he was the least likely to settle down. I mean, she wasn't excitedly positive about any of them being marriage material, but I seem to recall her saying that Sloan was the wild card."

It was true, Kendall remembered. Sloan had never been like Jace, who claimed he wanted a woman and a family. Or like Galen, who thought he wanted to go back to school to pick up another specialty. Or Falcon, who just wanted to stay unconnected, enjoying his life as a thinker and a poet and a rebel. Or Dante and Tighe, who were determined to get out on the rodeo circuit, as soon as they were all freed of the grip the past had on Rancho Diablo.

But Sloan had married her, almost faster than she'd ever imagined a man might want to be wed. "I never thought about that. Sloan was the dedicated loner."

"Not for long, it seems," Nadine said with a gentle smile. "Seems he's more like a wolf, mating for life."

Kendall looked at her sons. "It's hard for me to compromise sometimes."

"Of course, dear. Compromising one's independence isn't really compromise, though," Mavis told her. "It's more like reinforcing."

Reinforcing. She'd never thought of it that way.

"It's like you build each other up, fill in each other's weaknesses," Corinne said. "He's not looking for a namby-pamby woman, Kendall. He wouldn't have married you if he hadn't loved your fire and your strength. I'd say that's exactly what attracted Sloan the most."

Kendall stood. She gathered up her purse and diaper bag, and the ladies helped her strap the babies into their stroller. "I can't thank you enough for helping me to see this another way."

"No trouble at all," Corinne said, beaming. "It's

what we love to do. Let me go get your book. You'll enjoy it, I just know. And when you get to the chapter on the infamous magic wedding dress that all the Callahan brides have worn, you just go ahead and ask Fiona about that." Corinne's eyes sparkled. "I believe she has it tucked away for the next wedding at Rancho Diablo."

"I know about the magic wedding dress," Kendall said. "The legend says a bride sees her true love when she puts it on. Supposedly the gown came via Jonas's wife. Someone in Sabrina's family bought it from a gypsy, if I have the story details right."

"That's right, and all the Callahan brides got married twice. Once on Rancho Diablo land." Corinne went to retrieve the book, coming back a moment later to slip it into the diaper bag. "You just come back anytime you need a chat," she said. "We've always got a pot of tea on and cookies in the oven."

Kendall left, pushing her sons out into the beautiful sunny day, feeling suddenly as if everything was going to be all right.

Magical, in fact.

Chapter Nineteen

Sloan went to the ring of seven stones that his grandfather had said was their new home, which seemed like years ago now. He hadn't thought then that this endless, barren place would ever seem like home—not that he had a real one. He had the cabin, but that wasn't a home—not like what he wanted to have with Kendall and his boys.

"Much has changed," he said out loud, and the words carried away on the slight breeze. Sloan knelt, put his hand on the stone nearest him, feeling the day's heat still in its smoothness. "Even my heart changed."

Changed so much, in ways he could never have anticipated. Maybe Sloan's grandfather had known. Maybe he would never know the things the chief knew. But he wanted to remain on the journey, walking the path set before him.

And he wanted to stay married to his wife.

He lit the small cache of sticks set in the middle of the stone circle. After a moment the flame caught, deepening to an orange hue in the tiny pyre. He'd not been back since his grandfather had brought him and his siblings here. This fire had not been lit since then. Sloan had half expected not even to find it.

Yet it was, a calm testament to permanence in the canyons. He breathed in deep, let the peace wash over him.

It felt good to be home.

His grandfather stepped out from a nearby cave, almost as if he'd expected him to come.

"Grandfather," Sloan said.

"Sloan Chacon Callahan. You are here for answers. And peace for your spirit."

He smiled at the chief. His grandfather never seemed to change. That long, flowing hair somehow stayed dark; his face untouched by time, his muscles and bones strong. "I want everything to be right."

Running Bear nodded. "Looking for answers *is* right. I saw your sons in the hospital." He smiled. "They will make you strong."

"Sometimes they make me weak," Sloan said, and the two men squatted near the fire to talk. "I fear for them. They're so helpless."

"But their mother is a warrior. As you are." He waved a hand over the fire and the flame leaped a bit, stretching toward the darkening sky.

"She is," Sloan acknowledged, "and she scares me, too. I want to protect her, but that isn't something she wants from me."

The chief shrugged. "In many societies, the women are strong warriors. It's a good thing. You would know real fear if she was weak."

Sloan hadn't thought of it that way. "I can't keep her safe here, but she doesn't want to leave. Kendall wants to be here with me. She's a fighter."

"So let her fight. Life is a fight," Running Bear said. "Would you rather she give up?"

"No." He loved her spirit.

"Your sons are fighters. They were born early, but they thrived anyway. And in the future, they will be very much like their grandfather."

Sloan stared at his uncle. "How do you know this?"

"We are warriors. We protect, we serve. You expect them to be any different than either of their grandfathers?"

"I don't know," Sloan said. "They're so tiny. I can't imagine them as men."

His grandfather laughed. "Then you're not looking. Not listening to their spirits. Next time you hold them, look into their eyes. See the spirits of warriors inside them."

That scared him. He wanted to protect them—but he knew the chief was telling him he could not. They, too, would choose their own paths. But they would be strong.

Like their mother.

"The hardest thing you will ever do is accept that you are only to guard them now. Later, you will give them away to their destiny."

Sloan nodded. "I understand now."

"There is nothing to fear. We are all our destinies."

"I know." It was going to be hard, but he knew now. "Thank you."

"You have done well. Your wife and sons are gifts to make you strong. You have kept the land safe."

"I don't know if I have. There's so much I don't understand." Sloan stared into the fire. "They're going to keep coming."

"Maybe," the chief said, "but that's all they can do. They don't know it, but they can never take back the past."

Sloan wished he had his grandfather's confidence.

But then again, he and his siblings were strong. And they were fighters, with strong spirits. He knew that now.

Sloan watched his grandfather walk to the edge of the canyons. And then he simply disappeared. A war cry echoed in the distance.

Sloan let the fire die out and rode away.

KENDALL DISMISSED the bodyguards for the night, wanting time alone with her babies, and her husband if he came home. She hoped with all her heart he would. More than anything, she wanted to talk to him, work things out with Sloan, tell him how much she loved him.

She didn't know if he would come home to her. A lot of darkness had touched their brief marriage.

She put the babies in their cribs, smiling at her sons as they snuggled down into their blankets, worn out by the car ride. They were so sweet, so darling that she didn't know how she could have ever thought she wouldn't want children. They'd completely changed her heart, and her life.

Like their father.

Kendall turned around when she heard the front door open. Sloan walked into the nursery, tall and broad-shouldered, his face set in firm lines. Her heart leaped with hope.

"The babies just fell asleep," Kendall said.

He came to look into the cribs. "They're strong. Like their mother."

She looked at him, studying his face. "I've been wondering."

"About?"

"Us." She took Sloan's hand, and when he didn't

resist her, led him down the hall to the den. "Are you happy?"

He sat on the couch and pulled her into his lap. "Yes. You make me happy."

"I do?" She loved hearing those words, felt hope grow inside her.

He kissed her, long and slowly. "Yes. You make me happier than I've ever been in my life. You're part of my family, part of my soul and part of me."

Tears jumped into her eyes. "I didn't expect to hear you say something like that."

"I won't forget to tell you in the future."

She took a deep breath. "Sloan, I know I'm not—"

"You are," he said, kissing her again before she could finish her sentence. "You're everything to me. I've been afraid to know that. I wanted to keep you safe. But that's not what is best. Your spirit needs to be free."

She smiled. "I love you."

"I love you so much. I don't ever want to lose you." He kissed her, and Kendall felt her heart soar. "I think the problem is that we didn't get married in the customary way."

"What do you mean?"

"We got married thinking perhaps we would get divorced after the babies were born. I should never have made that deal with you. I just wanted you any way I could get you."

"Can we fix it?" Kendall asked, wondering what was on her husband's mind.

"Marry me again. With our friends and our family around. And our boys, of course."

She kissed him, filled with joy and thankfulness. "I think that's a wonderful idea."

"You would do it?"

She smiled. "Miss the chance to tie you down a second time? It's reinforcement."

Sloan looked at his wife, heard her words. Remembered that his grandfather had told them a long time ago that a chain could be broken if the weakest link wasn't reinforced.

He wasn't weak, not anymore. He had Kendall and his sons, and he was strong.

He held his wife against his chest, feeling the wolf settle inside him with a sense of contentment and peace he knew would last for the rest of his life.

He had found his destiny.

Epilogue

Kendall and Sloan were married at Rancho Diablo on a Saturday night at the end of July, in a ceremony so beautiful that Kendall felt a new bond bloom to life between her and husband. But she'd known that, the minute she'd donned the magic wedding dress Fiona had urged her to try on.

She'd seen Sloan the instant she'd stepped into the splendid gown, seemingly so real she'd actually thought he was in the room.

He wasn't. But he was in her heart, a part of her she would never be without.

She walked down the aisle, given away by Xav, who'd been convinced to come out of his canyon exile long enough to escort her to her husband's side. She'd asked Fiona to be her matron of honor, which had thrilled the older woman. Kendall couldn't imagine a more fitting person to stand up with her.

Jonas and the rest of the Callahans came to Rancho Diablo for the wedding, so it was a huge affair with lots of laughter and joy, and sweet reminiscing. It was wonderful for everyone to be "home" again, and joy washed over Kendall that her marriage gave everyone a reason to be together.

It wouldn't be for long—and the ranch was heavily guarded—but being married with her family and friends here meant the world to her. And Kendall was so thankful to Sloan for somehow knowing that she needed this time to renew and celebrate their vows to each other.

In the midst of the celebration, in a quiet moment together, Sloan squeezed her hand, and she looked up at him with a secret smile. "I love you," she told him.

"I'm very thankful for that." Sloan kissed her fingers. "I still can hardly believe that I won such a wonderful woman."

"You *are* lucky," she teased.

"I have three wonderful people in my life. That's a blessing," he told her.

"I fell in love with you the moment you made love to me. But I don't think I realized that love could grow deeper."

He smiled, and kissed her. "I fell in love with you when you stomped into my campsite wearing those heels and that white skirt."

"You did not," Kendall said, laughing. "You didn't even know I was there."

He smiled again. "I know you're here now. And that's all that matters to me."

It was all that mattered to her, too. They went and got their babies from the aunts who were passing them around, each eager for a chance to spoil the newest Callahans. Kendall and Sloan held their sons, falling in love even more deeply, and when they heard the thunder of the Diablos running in the canyons, celebrating the spirits that would always be a part of them, they